Twelve in the _____

A racing thriller

By

Charlie De Luca

www. charliedeluca.co.uk

To my family with love x

Edited by My Cup of Tea Press

Chapter 1

It was a bright Autumn afternoon as Jed Cavendish made his way into the weighing room at Uttoxeter races. He was rushing to get there before the forty-five-minute deadline, but full of anticipation for his first race meeting as a professional jockey. He was tall, dark and he liked to think rather handsome. At least several former girlfriends had described him as such. He was five feet eleven inches or so and his rangy build made him appear taller, so much so, people who met him were constantly surprised about his choice of career. That was until they realised he had endless legs and although broad, carried very little flesh on his frame. Being a National Hunt jockey was the only thing he had ever wanted to really do, ever since he had accompanied his grandfather to the races as a child and been entranced by the bright jockeys' silks, the noise and glamour of the smart crowds who laughed, smoked and drank from champagne flutes, as they cheered their horses.

Although, he was the younger son and it was his elder brother who was destined to carry on the family business, there were still expectations weighing down on his shoulders. His parents did not really approve of his career as a jockey and hoped that it was a passion that would soon burn out. However, he knew differently. Even if he couldn't ride, he knew that he wanted to work with horses in some capacity, but racing had got under his skin ever since he had ridden in his first amateur race and experienced the thrill of race riding. It was then that his fate was sealed. So, he had persuaded his father that he would merely delay joining the family business for a year and try to make a go of it as a professional jockey. The plan was that he would

4

prove so successful in his chosen career that his family would relent and forget about their expectations. The Cavendish family arranged lavish weddings and parties, renting out their home, Cavendish Hall, for this purpose. With his elder brother, Hugh, now practically running the whole show single-handedly, Jed felt that he should be given the freedom to pursue his own career. Since he had ridden out his claim, as a conditional jockey with Harry Smythe in Cheltenham, he'd had six months to apply for a professional licence and it had been an easy decision to make. When Harry had unexpectedly died of cancer, he had come back North to try his hand as a professional. Poor Harry, one minute he had complained of frequent indigestion, the next, he had just weeks to live. Still, it also made Jed determined to follow his dream, as life was just too short otherwise.

Having taken this monumental step, which risked incurring the permanent disapproval of his family, he now realised that he had to deliver. He had to show Cavendish Senior that this passion was not a short-lived pipe dream but could actually become a successful and viable career. He was deep in thought as he rushed and began to change into his jockey's colours for the first race. He greeted his elderly valet, George, who ran the weighing room like clockwork, with a nod. George glanced at his watch and raised merely raised an eyebrow at his lateness, rather indulgently like a good natured uncle. He served his 'young gentlemen' as he liked to call them, with unswerving loyalty and pride, hardly ever criticising or pointing out any misdemeanours.

Jed was one the last to arrive. The other jockeys were all there in various stages of undress, excited by the prospect of a good afternoon's racing. Eddie O'Neill, a jockey from Cork and good friend grinned broadly at Jed.

'Now what time d'ya call this? Did you have something better to do, eh?'

Jed grinned back. 'Well, I'm here now. Had a bit of a late one last night...'

'Not that posh Arabella again was it? I thought you and she were history...'

Jed shrugged. 'So did I, but we met up, had a few drinks and then I ended up at hers, you know how it is...'

Eddie grinned and elbowed him before groaning. 'I need the bloody loo again. I took some of tablets, all natural they are, to keep me weight down and it's working too damned well. It's just that now I'm peeing for England, Scotland and Ireland, so I am.' He held up a packet of sky blue pills. 'All legal, so don't you be worrying.'

'What's in them?' asked Tristan, who clearly was worried.

Eddie peered at the label. 'Dandelion, ginger and parsley. Probably useless, maybe it's all in me head but I'm still busting to pee!'

With that he rushed off to relieve himself. The lads laughed and made some ribald remarks at Eddie's expense. They probably all suspected that the tablets were diuretics and could well be on the BHA banned list, but Eddie was a grown man and an experienced jockey, so he knew the rules and would have to take any consequences. Still, at least it was only tablets, some of the others went to much greater lengths to win their battle with the scales. It was well known that jockeys resorted to laxatives, saunas and even some to illegal drugs to make the weights, especially the flat jockeys. Eddie was smaller than Jed, but naturally a stockier build so did struggle on occasions to make the weights. Thank goodness, National Hunt jockeys could generally get away with ten or eleven stone rather the unobtainable eight stone or so required for most flat jockeys.

As Jed pulled on the red and yellow silks of his first runner, which had been neatly laid out by George, he heard a buzzing coming from nearby. At first, he thought it was an insect, maybe a bee or

6

bluebottle that had found its way into the weighing room, but as it was early autumn, he dismissed the idea. Then the sound of a country and western classic, Tammy Wynette's 'Stand by your Man' assaulted his ears, accompanied by groans from the entire room.

'Answer your fucking phone, mate, or better still turn the bloody thing off!'

'Shit, what a rubbish ring tone. Answer it!' cried another.

Jed fumbled around as he traced the noise to Ed's coat pocket. He glanced at the clock as he did so, realising that it was just before the thirty-minute cut off point when all jockeys had to turn off their mobiles and hand them in before the start of the afternoon's racing. Switching phones to silent was no good, mobiles had to be definitely turned off thirty minutes before the meeting and given to a staff member, only to be returned and switched on again at the end of racing. These were the British Horseracing Authority rules and were designed to prevent corruption. To disobey the ruling meant a fine and repeated infringements were frowned upon and could result in disciplinary action. He pulled out the silver mobile handset and jabbed at the buttons frantically, trying to turn the wretched thing off. There, that should do it. But instead he heard a disembodied voice say. 'That you?' Without thinking he put the handset to his ear.

'Twelve in the sixth.'

Jed was about to ask what the hell he was talking about when the call cleared abruptly. He shook his head and turned the bloody thing off and placed the phone and his own in the basket, ready to be handed in to the security officer for safe keeping. His valet, George, looked pointedly at him.

'It's not my phone. It's Eddie's but no worries it's switched off now and there's mine too.' He inclined his head at the basket which was filling up with the jockey's mobiles. Not to worry. He'd tell Eddie later. He was soon distracted by Jake Horton and Tristan

Davies asking him if he had seen the presenter of the new television programme 'Racing Days.' Felicity Hill was the new face of the programme and following on the recent popularity of the sport, she was appointed as a way of gaining a new, youthful audience. An ex glamour model with little knowledge of horses but with a very pleasing figure and confidential almost flirtatious manner when interviewing the jockeys and connections, the jury was very much out on her success to date. Jed rather liked the old presenter, Penny Morris. She was the wrong side of fifty, wore an odd assortment of clothes and was said to resemble a sort of country bag lady on occasions, but she knew horses inside out and the jockeys and trainers trusted her. Jed felt saddened about her departure and the way she had been unceremoniously swept aside for a new, younger model.

'Well, I think she's a bit of alright that Felicity,' explained Jake. 'Great looking girl like that, she's bound to introduce new blood to the sport. I wouldn't kick her out of bed, anyways. Better than those old presenters.' He screwed up his face. 'Penny always reminded me of my nan.'

There were many comments and laughter at this. Tristan shook his head and leapt to Penny's defence.

'Well, at least she knew about horses and we all trusted her. This Felicity doesn't know one end of a horse from the other. She thinks a hock is a type of wine and she asked me other day about what P means in the formbook. I had to explain that P stood for 'pulled up' not poorly, as she suggested. And she's a bit too flirty for my liking. She was all over Eddie like a rash.'

'Terrible taste, stupid bitch,' muttered an older, rather sour faced jockey called Gary McKay. He spat the words out with real venom. This might have been funny if one of the others had said it, but Gary had a way of handing out nasty jibes that were calculated to hurt. He also had a reputation of 'rough riding' and doing anything to win by whipping his horse too hard or barging the other jockeys out of position. Eddie had sort of taken over from Gary as stable jockey for a successful yard when Gary was injured, and he had never quite recovered his position in the racing world. Eddie got the rides and did so well that there was no place for Gary. He did not have the security of being a stable jockey these days, riding for anyone who would hire him, so probably did have a grudge against Eddie. Still, racing was like that, Jed reflected, and Eddie's sunny personality as well as his superior skill with horses, made him a much better prospect than the surly Scot. However, Gary seemed to have developed a real chip on his shoulder as a result.

Eddie came back at this point and flushed pink at the innuendo and comments he received about the new presenter. Following weighing in, Jed joined in with good humour, just as the bell rang and it was time for the jockeys to go into the parade ring. The telephone call was forgotten.

Jed's mount in the first race was the unpromising Eldorado, an unplaced four-year-old gelding who had shown enough stamina over the flat to be tried over hurdles for a season. Jed touched his cap to the owners, as was the tradition. The florid faced pair, who were all sun tans and gold bracelets, were excitedly taking in the atmosphere of the parade ring whilst the trainer Pat McGuire gave Jed his instructions, though these were worryingly brief.

'Just get around in one piece,' was all that Pat could say. 'It's more of a training ride, see.' Jed's heart sank as he assumed that the horse was little schooled and sadly this proved to be the case. Still, despite struggling with the brakes and his mount's unnerving habit of veering to the left over fences, he managed a creditable fifth. He felt the blood pumping through his veins as he wiped the mud from his goggles, the familiar rush of euphoria flushing through him. Then it was down to earth with a bump as he had a no hoper in the second, who deposited him at the third fence, and another in the fourth race who had to be pulled up due to lameness. He sat out the fifth race and looked forward to his more promising ride in the sixth race.

This horse was the grey gelding, High Society. As well as being a stunning creature, he was trained by a relatively new female trainer, Lydia Fox, who was a likeable woman, but something of an unknown quantity in racing circles as she was a newcomer. She had a small number of horses but seemed to know exactly what she was doing and was a real horsewoman. It was just a pity that her career had been slow to take off and Jed had to put this down to conservatism within the industry. She was without doubt talented, so Jed was, therefore, particularly keen to do well for her. High Society was 7-1, having been placed a couple of times and Lydia seemed to fancy his chances. A slim, attractive brunette with a weather-beaten complexion, she advised Jed to keep him in the pack and then pick them off one by one from half a furlong out if the big grey had any running left in him. The owners hadn't been able to attend, so it was just her and Jed in the parade ring. Lydia cast her experienced eyes over the other horses as they were led round.

'Eddie O'Neill's horse, Happy Days looks well and is the red-hot favourite,' she commented, 'and Charlie Durrant's ride is also a threat, as is Gary McKay's mount Monseignor.' Her eyes were earnest as she studied her own horse. 'But High Society has really has been working well at home, so he could be in with a shout. This is your first professional season, isn't it?'

Jed nodded. 'Yeah, thought I'd like to give it a go as a professional, for a change. Can't let the other lads have all the fun, after all.'

Lydia grinned. 'Well, let's see how you do, but I'm hoping to expand this year, so might be calling on you to ride a few for me. I usually use Charlie or Tristan, but they are in such demand, there is an opening. So, give it your best shot.'

Jed beamed his spirits lifting as he looked into Lydia's honest and open face. She was right to say that Charlie Durrant and his mate Tristan Davies were very busy these days. Their careers had gone from strength to strength. This did leave something of a vacuum, which left space for him. It was exactly the opportunity he was looking for and was determined not to foul things up. He studied Charlie's mount, intent on keeping the bright bay horse in his sights. He also committed Eddie's navy colours with red seams to memory as well as Gary McKay's black and orange hoops. Gary's horse looked a little small for his liking, so he predicted it would be him, Eddie or Charlie fighting it out at the end.

Jed positioned the big grey horse carefully with space to manoeuvre and with only four horses ahead of him in the first circuit, he kept his eyes firmly on Eddie's navy clad back. High Society was full of running and as he had thought, had been well schooled. The horse was jumping well and cleanly. He wiped his mud spattered goggles as he kept up with the leaders and avoided getting himself boxed in. The thundering hooves and the feel of the cool air, combined with the earthy smell of the turf enveloped him like a comfort blanket. At this moment he was surer than he'd ever been that this was the life he really wanted. He was never happier than when he was race riding. He would wither and die working with his father and brother, but to convince the old man and keep him off his back, he needed results and for that he would have to keep his wits about him and take his chances when they came.

They moved into the second and final circuit of the two mile race and he positioned his mount on the outside in readiness for the final push. He moved up the field, passing Gary McKay on his bright bay, tracking Eddie who was now in second position behind Charlie's Durrant's horse which appeared to be tiring. With one hurdle left, he decided to see what High Society had left in the tank and he pressed his legs against the big grey's sides and pushed on. The grey responded and made a huge leap over the last fence landing just behind Eddie's bay horse. Charlie was really pushing his horse and muttering encouragements, but it was clear that the animal was a spent force and was beginning to trail. Meanwhile, Gary McKay was coming back. He could see him riding forcefully in the last few strides. Jed focused and urged High Society on towards the finish line, riding with his hands, heels and heart, rocking his body back and forward and raising his whip. He gave his horse one sharp smack. In a blur of colour and cheers, Eddie's navy figure remained tantalisingly ahead, and Gary's horse rallied to just beat him. Damn. In the end he was pipped into third place.

Eddie turned around, his face split by his grin. Jed grinned back still exhilarated despite the disappointment of losing. Neither he nor his mount could have given any more.

'Well ridden mate. Better luck next time. Almost a professional job.'

It was a well worn joke between the two of them. Eddie was forever bemoaning Jed's gentleman/ amateur status, as someone with private means, except that now this season he was one of them. He felt a surge of excitement at the thought. Sadly, Gary was not so pleased and swore and cursed at Eddie. What a bad sport! Back in the winner's enclosure, Lydia watched the argument between Eddie and Gary with interest. She seemed pleased with High Society's run though. Jed drank in the praise and promise of further rides. As he removed the saddle from his steaming mount to weigh in, he spotted someone staring and frowning. It was a face he recognised. Darren Francis. What was he doing here? Darren Francis's career and subsequent fall from grace was legendary in racing circles. He had been an up and coming jockey until his form became erratic and he was eventually suspended for pulling races. Although he had tried to come back, the racing community had lost trust in him and he struggled to find work. He hadn't been seen in a long time. He looked quite well, his blond hair was expensively tousled, and he wore a smart looking suit, so he must be working. Darren's gaze was clearly fixed on someone and he realised it was Eddie. First Gary and now Darren. Gary was clearly outraged at being beaten and as for Darren, probably, he had put his money on Gary's ride too, Jed decided. The world of racing was full of disgruntled punters, that was for sure. He shrugged and gave the matter no more thought.

As he made his way to the weighing room, he saw Eddie pause to speak briefly to the new presenter Felicity Hill. He took in her highlighted blonde hair, tight clothing and the way she had of clutching Eddie's arm and staring wide eyed at him. Eddie flushed and then snatched off his saddle and cloth and walked back to the weighing room. Felicity's gaze followed his progress which made him think that the rumours about their relationship must be true. It was only then that Jed noticed that the white saddle cloth Eddie was carrying had the number '12' boldly displayed in black. Something resonated and he remembered the call to Eddie's mobile, realising with a pang that he had forgotten to pass on the message. Dimly, his brain tried to connect the two pieces of information. *Twelve in the sixth.* Twelve of what in the sixth of what? It could mean anything. He was annoyed with himself for forgetting to pass the message on. Never mind, whoever it was who rang was bound to call back if it was important and he had a dinner party to go to. His sister, Milly, spurred on by an addiction to cookery programmes, had invited him to a dinner party to 'make up the numbers' as she termed it. This usually meant that she would have invited a spare female who she thought might be suitable for him. Jed's idea about suitable and his sister's, had rarely coincided to date, so he was expecting to have to politely extricate himself from whoever she had lined up for him. But he was at least looking forward to seeing Milly and after a good afternoon's racing with a third place in the bag, at least he had something to celebrate. Milly understood about his passion for racing and there was no one else he wanted to share his success with.

He left the racecourse, exchanging good natured 'craic' with Eddie, who seemed none the worse for his row with Gary. Jed drove home in good spirits, in anticipation of an entertaining evening, the phone call completely forgotten.

Chapter 2

Imogen James ran a hand through her unruly brown curls, added mascara, a slick of lip gloss and straightened her red woollen dress which showed off her slender figure. She added black long boots with a slight heel, a squirt of Vera Wang's 'Princess' perfume and surveyed herself in the mirror. Her black rimmed glasses made her look too brainy, so she removed them which instantly improved her reflection. Or was it just that everything was slightly blurred? It was hard to tell. She thought she looked stylish, like she hadn't tried too hard which she was exactly the look she was aiming for. She was worried about accepting the invitation from her boss or more accurately, his partner Milly, and wanted to look as casual as she could. She knew from Milly's keen gaze and the way she had dropped her younger brother's name repeatedly into the conversation, that she was invited as a potential partner for him. Of course, Milly had termed it 'making up the numbers'. She was far too well-mannered to be more obvious. Imogen felt a flush of embarrassment at the thought. As the invite had come from the partner of her good-natured boss, she had felt it would be churlish to refuse. She found herself at such a low ebb after her long-term boyfriend, Sam had decided to go travelling for an indefinite period, that she had found herself glad at the opportunity to socialise. It had to be better than watching Saturday night TV alone with a tub of Ben and Jerry's ice cream for company. Besides, Milly was interesting and quick witted so maybe her brother would be the same? She could always talk shop with Jack and discuss his ideas for developing the research profile of the team if all else failed.

Jack and Milly lived in a large Edwardian terraced house near York racecourse, which was also handy for the University. She took a deep breath as she balanced a hastily bought bottle of wine in the crook of her arm and rang the doorbell. A gust of heat and light welcomed her as Jack opened the door and ushered her inside. She grinned feeling suddenly rather shy at seeing him at home away from the usual office environment. She heard the chatter of voices and was embraced by the warmth and smell of something delicious. There was no turning back now.

There were two other couples; Simon another lecturer friend of Jack's and his fresh-faced girlfriend Phoebe, and Cassie, Milly's Head of Department, who was with her balding and harassed looking husband, Malcolm. Jack made introductions and handed Imogen a glass of red wine. Milly appeared flushed and anxious, hastily hugging her before dashing back into the kitchen to sort out the cooking. Imogen made polite conversation, adding that she worked with Jack and explained her research. She was aware that Jed had not arrived and was just beginning to relax, thinking he wasn't coming when the doorbell rang out, loud and shrill. Jack went to answer it and came back with a tall, lean man with dark curls and prominent cheekbones. He had the look of a macho male model saved from being too perfect by his slightly crooked nose and the craggy hollows to his face. Milly dashed over to greet him, and he kissed her on both cheeks in a continental fashion. Milly introduced the others and then turned to Imogen.

'Imogen this is Jed, Jed, Imogen. Imogen works with Jack who says he couldn't manage without her. She has a fantastic brain,' Milly explained. Imogen flushed as fudge coloured eyes scrutinised her. Milly hadn't meant it, she was sure, but it made her feel like her intellect was highlighted in order to make up for her appearance. Instantly, she felt at a disadvantage as Jed studied her. She felt like he could see into the furthest reaches of her soul.

'I'm sure you're not doing justice to Imogen at all,' he added, as though he liked what he saw. 'So, you work at the University like Milly, do you?'

Imogen nodded and went on to explain about the complex research Jack was conducting.

'It's a longitudinal study about the long-term effects of prescription and over the counter drugs. Ground breaking stuff really.'

Jed merely raised a sardonic eyebrow. Clearly not an academic then.

Imogen tried not to squint at him, but it was hard to reciprocate his scrutiny since she opted not to wear her spectacles. She tried very hard not to stare.

'So, what is it that you do?' she asked.

'Well, I am a jockey. National Hunt. This is my first professional season and my first race meeting as a professional was today. I came third in one race, so I'm celebrating.' Imogen couldn't help noticing how his face lit up as he said this and went on to discuss his rides at Uttoxeter.

'Course, dad wants Jed to go into the family business, but Jed's always loved horses and riding, so it was never going to end well...' Milly smiled indulgently. She was several years older than her brother and clearly adored him.

Phoebe stood up to chat to Jed. That figured. She had dirty blonde hair and had the no nonsense briskness of a horse woman.

'Oh. I love a day at the races. Ridden many winners?'

'Yes, seventy-nine. I have ridden out my claim as a conditional and have just taken my professional licence out. I've given myself a year to prove that I can make it.' Jed explained. 'So,

I'm going to give it my all.' He smiled at Phoebe who smirked back, much to her boyfriend's irritation.

'Isn't horse racing terribly cruel with all those horses dying in the Grand National and jockeys whipping them within an inch of their lives?' asked Cassie, Milly's boss from Psychology. She had a loud, self-important voice that boomed out.

Jed studied her, a slight smile playing on his lips. 'No, not at all. It's very well regulated. Thoroughbred horses are born to race and truly love it. They are so much bigger and stronger than humans, you couldn't force them to do anything against their will.'

Cassie sniffed. 'Yes, but we humans have much bigger brains that we can use to manipulate them, so it's hardly a valid argument.'

'Hmm. I take it you've never actually ridden? Horses never do anything they don't want to do, believe me.'

Cassie pressed on, ignoring Milly's attempts to change the subject, oblivious to the sudden change of atmosphere in the room. There was a hush as everyone waited to see which way the argument would go. Phoebe had backed away and made no attempt to assist Jed. She was clearly as intimidated by Cassie as Milly seemed to be. Simon looked to be enjoying himself hugely whilst Jack looked rather ill at ease. Milly was near to tears. Sadly, Cassie was unaware of the tension and stood up to face Jed.

'And there's all the betting scandals. You're not telling me that you haven't heard of horses being doped with wholescale cheating and bookies running the show?'

Jed glanced at his sister.

'Well, like all sports you always get one or two bad apples who spoil it for everyone else, but I do believe in the overall integrity of the sport, otherwise I wouldn't be in it.' He smiled. 'You should come to the races with Milly. I'll even send you some tickets and show you round. I'm sure you'd enjoy it.'

Cassie muttered something under her breath about being far too busy and her husband Malcolm asked if Jed had ever raced against Tony McCoy, the champion jockey who had now retired. Cassie glared at him for showing an interest as Jed explained that, yes, he had raced against the great man.

'Of course, he's retired now but he is a fabulous chap and a consummate professional.' Cassie realised all the room was against her, including her husband and decided to back down. Milly beamed as calm reigned once again. Imogen saw that Jed had come alive defending his sport. He had a sort of energy about him that radiated out of every pore. Without her glasses it was hard to tell if he was good looking, but he had a dynamism about him and a beautiful, cultured voice. She had a feeling that the evening was going to be anything but dull with him around.

Jack decided to distract Cassie by encouraging her to talk about her research and she droned on and on about control groups, how hard it was to get anything through the Ethics Committees these days and how unruly and ignorant the current undergraduates were. She then went on to ask if Milly's menu was gluten free, as she had recently discovered that she was gluten intolerant. She clearly hadn't told Milly, whose face fell.

Imogen had drunk quite a lot of wine to calm her nerves. This made her feel brave enough to address Jed about his verbal sparring with Cassie.

'Nicely done, disaster averted.'

Jed grinned and took a sip of wine.

'I think I've just been diagnosed as Cassie intolerant, I don't know about you,' he muttered, casting a mutinous look at Cassie who had launched into a list of things she could eat, settling on a few miserable vegetables. 'Appalling woman.'

Imogen laughed rather wildly.

Jed clearly sensed that he had an ally. 'You don't seem like an academic.'

'I'm not quite sure how to interpret that...'

'Well. I meant it as a compliment.' He gave her an assessing sort of a look. 'Why don't we play nicely for a little while, eat and then bugger off to the pub. I know you were invited as a 'spare' female, but don't worry I'm not hitting on you. I am coming out in hives in such close proximity to Cassie. If you don't come too, I'll be tempted to tell her about all my escapades on the hunting field, watching hounds tearing foxes limb from limb and being bloodied as a child.'

'You wouldn't?'

Jed nodded, a slow smile spreading over his face.

Imogen didn't want to appear rude to her hosts, but then separating Jed and Cassie was a very good plan especially as she kept glowering at Jed. Cassie was Milly's head of Department and she had probably only invited her out of politeness. A discussion about fox hunting would probably cause a riot as Cassie was bound to be an anti if the earlier conversation was anything to go by. Imogen abhorred the thought of blood sports too, but discussing such a topic would be rather like throwing a match into a box of fireworks.

'Did you really get bloodied? I thought that sort of practice was outlawed nowadays?'

She heard the humour in his voice.

'Nah. I've never actually been hunting. I like foxes too much.' He put his fingers to his lips. 'Ssh, don't tell anyone. So, are we still off out?'

She hesitated but only for a second.

'You're on.'

At coffee, Jed whispered to his sister and they left.

They sat quietly in 'The George Inn'. Milly had looked panicked, but also rather pleased at the same time when Jed had kissed her and announced that he and Imogen were leaving together after the meal. She was probably thinking that for once her matchmaking has proved successful.

Jed plonked a glass of wine down in front of Imogen.

'How did Milly persuade you to come along? I hope she didn't go on about how her baby brother was still single and hasn't managed to meet the right girl?'

'Yes, it was something like that. But I came along because of Jack really. I work with him and he invited me. That's it.' She hadn't the heart to reveal what Jack had said, which was that Milly's brother was a 'great bloke' who had left a trail of broken hearts behind him and needed the love of a good woman to settle down. Jack had decided that he definitely wasn't Imogen's type, but she had been intrigued. How could Jack know that, when she hardly knew herself what her type was? Probably, he had meant that Jed wasn't an academic, but then that was a very good thing. Sam was and look what happened there...

Jed studied her. 'Well, I'm glad we made the great escape from Cassie, anyway. Perhaps, we should start again. What do you

21

like to do when you're not slaving away over statistics and poring over data.'

Imogen was pleased he had remembered. 'I am into fitness, love the cinema, read avidly and am into taekwondo.'

'Really? Now that does surprise me. What belt are you up to?'

Damn. Imogen normally never revealed this to anyone. It just caused complications and all sorts of macho challenges she could well do without.

'Oh, it's not really about that. It's more to do with self defence, discipline, that sort of thing.'

'Well, well well....' His phone suddenly started ringing. He held up his hand as though stopping traffic. He silenced the phone and put it back in his pocket and was just about to speak when it started ringing again almost immediately. Jed grimaced and answered it this time.

'OK. Hi. Right.' Imogen watched as Jed suddenly became serious and began pacing up and down, his expression becoming more and more tense. 'What, you're not making any sense mate. Eddie? Eddie? Where are you, what's going on? Right. I'm on my way.' After a while, Jed stood up and began putting his coat on. He held out both his hands in a helpless gesture. 'I'm so sorry. It's my friend Ed. He sounds in a bad way. I think he's in some sort of trouble. I'll have to go and meet up with him.' He downed his drink and looked at her earnestly. 'Look. It's not an excuse, honestly. I'd like to meet up again. We should definitely go out on a proper date. I'll be in touch.'

With that he disappeared, and Imogen was left sipping her wine, avoiding the pitying glances of the barman and the other customers. Bloody hellfire and damnation! The thing was, despite what Jack had thought, she had to admit she rather liked Jed. She wasn't fooled for a minute by his comment about going out on a proper date. How stupid did that make her feel? He was funny and intriguing and, she had to admit clearly a bit of a shit. Probably good looking too, if she had managed to see him clearly. She fished in her bag for her glasses and avoided the curious gaze of the barman. Well, she told herself, she had very likely had a lucky escape and she should feel relieved. She drank her wine, grabbed her coat and smiled bravely at the handful of customers, as she made her way out into the busy street. She was surprised to find that instead of feeling relieved about Jed's absence, she actually felt quite bereft.

Chapter 3

Eddie's timing was spectacularly bad Jed decided, as he drove the short distance to the health club that Ed frequented and where they had arranged to meet. He had found Imogen rather intriguing, not his type, but likeable and pretty, just the same. She had an intensity about her and would have been far prettier if she hadn't kept squinting. She seemed quite normal for an academic unlike Cassie, who represented the worst of the academic types, opinionated, bullish and downright rude. He had no idea why Milly put up with her, even if she was her boss.

His thoughts turned to the task in hand. Eddie had been almost incoherent when he rang whether from illness, drugs or alcohol it was hard to tell. He'd known Ed about three years now, they were not just colleagues but good mates. They'd started out together and shared the good times and the bad. There had been a lot of bad, but things had picked up and they were both reaping the benefits of hard work. Jed had no idea why Eddie had rung. He liked a drink and probably had got carried away celebrating his first win of the season he decided, but he knew deep down there was something else. Eddie had sounded breathless and softly spoken almost, as though he was worried about being overheard. He also sounded, and he baulked at the description, scared too. He wondered if it was anything to do with the argument with Gary McKay but dismissed it as Eddie wasn't the sort to let professional jealousies get him down. Then he wondered about his relationship with Felicity Hill then decided that it was unlikely to be a source of conflict. Still, if Eddie was just drunk and having a laugh, he'd be annoyed as he had been forced to leave the warmth of the pub and the company of a pretty girl to meet him.

He arrived at 'Hot Bodies' at about half past nine. The car park was fairly empty and in the gathering gloom, he parked up and looked round for Eddie's car. He had recently bought himself a top of the range silver Golf. Jed drove around, but if it was there, he couldn't see it. As he entered the reception area, the smell of polish and stale sweat assailed him. The warmth was overwhelming. The receptionist directed him to the café and he ordered a latte from the bored looking young woman, sat down and waited. There was a group of young men fresh from the shower with gym bags on their shoulders, chatting as they walked. It was a Saturday night and he reckoned that most people would have better things to do than spend the evening at the gym. In the distance he saw a couple of dark haired men approach, convinced that the smaller man was Eddie, but when the man approached, he realised he was mistaken. He sipped his latte, checked his watch, then fished his mobile out of his pocket and rang Eddie. The call went straight to voicemail much to his annoyance. Bloody hell O'Neill, the least you could do is turn up! Time passed, he sipped his drink and glanced at his watch again. He realised he had been waiting for almost thirty minutes. What the hell was going on? He decided to wait ten minutes more and scrolled through some apps on his phone, checking the declarations for runners and riders for a race meeting next week. He drained his cup, wondered about ringing Milly to get Imogen's number and then decided that would be pushing it. He remembered Imogen's look of disbelief and disappointment when he made his excuses to leave, except they weren't excuses. He felt anger smart as he realised what she might think of him. He wandered into the reception area where a blonde, ponytailed woman was typing and checking membership cards.

'Hi there. I was meant to meet my mate Eddie O'Neill here. He's Irish, a bit smaller than me, dark haired, would have been here about eight o'clock, I think. Have you seen him leave?'

The girl chewed her nail and shook her head. 'I don't think I know him.' She smiled and turned back to her computer screen. 'Sorry.'

Jed smiled and fished in mobile out of his pocket. He tapped a few keys and found a BHA photo of Eddie in his work clothes of breeches and undershirt and showed it to the girl. She gave it a cursory glance.

'No, sorry. I haven't seen anyone who looks like him here.'

'OK. Thanks.'

What the hell was going on? Jed buttoned up his coat and left. He cursed inwardly, but also felt uneasy. Perhaps, Ed had gone off, probably met a mate, a girl, maybe even Felicity and forgotten to ring and tell him? Something didn't quite add up, but like a dream, the fragments kept spiralling out of reach. He glanced at his watch and toyed with the idea of going back to Milly's, but instantly Cassie's sour face came to mind. Eddie lived out of York towards Walton, the heart of racing in Yorkshire, where he was stable jockey to Kieron McLoughlin. He may as well drive there and see if he had decided to go straight home instead. Then, he would undoubtedly give him a piece of his mind for ruining his evening.

Outside the city the roads petered out into country lanes. It was almost completely black as the number of streetlights lessened. The night was clear, and the stars gleamed. A horrible sense of foreboding began to clutch at Jed's heart. Something just didn' feel right. He'd tried Eddie's mobile several times, but his calls just went to voicemail. In his rear-view mirror, he saw flashing lights and the sound of sirens, so he slowed to let the ambulance pass him. As he rounded the corner, he saw the accident it had been sent to. Lights flashed up ahead from the two police cars and fire engines that were helping some poor soul. The area had been cordoned off and a police car barred his way. Beyond the lights and sirens, his heart pounded as the lights illuminated the wreckage of an upturned silver golf. Eddie's golf. Realisation ebbed over him. That poor soul was Eddie.

Jed sipped the hideous coffee, dispensed from the hospital's drinks machine, whilst sitting down on a hard, blue plastic chair and waited. Eddie lay in intensive care and had multiple injuries. No one knew what had happened or whether another car was involved or not, just that Eddie's car had turned over and he'd had to be cut from the mangled wreckage. The police were investigating, but for now Eddie lay wired up to monitors whilst doctors assessed his injuries. They were mainly to his head and neck. The hospital had contacted Eddie's parents in Ireland and having gained consent to speak to Jed, actually shared very little information. Probably, they didn't know much themselves at this stage, he told himself. Another awful thought occurred to him. Supposing the injuries were very serious, too severe for discussion with a mere friend, the sort of conversations that were for the ears of family members only, spoken behind closed doors? The doctor Jed saw was cool, professional and very guarded. Wait and see seemed to be his mantra.

Jed had spent what felt like hours on the phone to Eddie's mother who was alternately crying or demanding further updates. She was hastily making arrangements to visit her son as soon as possible. No one had yet said that Eddie might not make it, so Jed took this a good sign, but had promised Mrs O'Neill he'd wait around to see what the prognosis was. He was half nodding off when his phone beeped. He pressed a few buttons and found that he had a message. He gasped when he realised it was from Eddie.

I've really ballsed things up. Need to speak to you asap. E

Jed checked the time it was sent and found it was before
Eddie's phone call to him in the pub. The signal must have been poor,
so poor it hadn't arrived until several hours later. He'd noticed it
before that sometimes depending on the network, text messages took
an age to arrive. A cold finger of alarm crept down his spine as
realisation jolted him as he put all the facts together in his tired brain.
Something wasn't right. There was the call in the changing room with
its strange message, *twelve in the sixth,* the message he hadn't passed
on, then the argument with Gary. Then Eddie had texted later to say
he'd 'ballsed' things up. Finally, he was involved in a serious car
crash. God, what the hell was going on? He tried to work through the
sequence of events. The call he had taken on Eddie's phone in the
changing room was clearly meant for Eddie and had arrived just
before the thirty minute cut off point. Disconnected pieces of
information kept floating into his consciousness. Eddie had won on
number twelve in the sixth race. Realisation crept down his spine,
snaking like an ice cube. Supposing number twelve wasn't meant to
have won? Perhaps, it was an instruction. Oh my God, that was it!
Thoughts spiralled round and round his head and he kept coming to
the same conclusion. Whichever way he looked at it, it seemed clear
that Eddie was meant to stop his mount, number twelve, Happy Days
from winning in the sixth race. Happy Days had won because Jed had
picked up Eddie's mobile instead. He hadn't passed the message on
and now Eddie was lying in hospital seriously injured, presumably as
some sort of payback or punishment for not complying with the
instruction. Maybe Gary McKay had realised and that was what they
were arguing about? He shook his head at the dreadful irony of the

name of the horse involved, Happy Days. It all made sense now. Eddie wasn't meant to win.

He waited in the airless corridor as the smell of disinfectant and polish filled his nostrils, studying the beige linoleum floor. He felt terrible guilt pressing down on his chest for not passing on the message. How he wished he had simply told Eddie. He would never have thought anything of it, the message was gobbledegook anyway. Eddie would have stopped his horse and that would be that and he would have been none the wiser. Now he knew what had happened he felt off kilter, shocked and saddened, like all his certainties about decency and professionalism were thrown into doubt. He would never have thought Eddie capable of such a thing as pulling a horse, but the questions circled round his brain in an endless painful loop and whichever way he looked at it, he kept coming to the same conclusion. What other explanation was there? He had to rethink everything he had ever known about his friend. Just how long had Eddie been paid to pull races and who had paid him to do it?

Eventually, the same sombre looking doctor came to find him.

'Mr Cavendish? I'm Dr French. Eddie has had a serious head injury and we have had to operate to relieve some of the pressure on his brain.' The grey eyes studied him, and Jed wondered what on earth it must be like to deal with such serious matters on a daily basis. 'We've put him into a medically induced coma whilst his brain recovers, and the swelling is reduced. That's the theory anyway.'

Shit. Jed didn't like the sound of that. He hadn't expected anything quite so serious. A coma? Questions ricocheted around his brain.

'God. How bad is it? I mean, will he make a full recovery?'

29

The grey eyes blinked steadily. 'It's hard to say with injuries like this, but I'm cautiously optimistic that he will. The next few hours will be crucial, but we must let nature takes its course.'

Jed nodded, relief bubbling. He shook Dr French's hand. 'Thank you so much. Can I see him?'

Dr French nodded. 'Just for a second.' He ushered Jed into a small, white room where Eddie lay, wired up to monitors and instruments which beeped and hummed all around him. He looked small, pale and vulnerable, his head encased in a huge bandage with bruises beginning to bloom, a faint purple splash across his forehead and another to one side of his cheek. His face was a mass of small cuts and abrasions. Yet, he looked like he might wake up at any time and explain that it was all a cruel prank, for he was known as a bit of a joker. Yet this was no joke. Jed found he was choking back tears. He was left in no doubt as to the seriousness of the situation. He grasped Eddie's hand in a helpless gesture, his mind in turmoil with questions to which he had no answers. Christ Eddie, what on earth have you got mixed up in?

Chapter 4

Imogen enjoyed being at work and loved the campus at York University even though, in contrast to the rest of the city, the buildings were new and functional. Her job as a research assistant appealed to her analytical, curious mind. She had studied biochemistry at York and then taken up the post working with Jack. He had obtained some funding to research the long-term effects of some common drugs. This involved interviewing subjects, assessing any side effects and analysing the data. The purpose was to see if long-term drug use changed the effects, whether the body adapted to the drugs, making them less effective and what the side effects over several years were. For example, they were studying the use of statins to control blood pressure and whether or not they continued to perform that function over time, or whether the body became inured to the effect. It was fascinating research and the thrill of seeking out answers to such tough questions really appealed to her. Jack was a good boss, encouraging, perceptive and very bright.

It was a Monday and business as usual. She had decided to put the evening she had spent with Jack and Milly down to experience and had concluded that Jed was a complete waste of space. She had found him attractive, but he clearly had issues. It was a long time since anyone had had to make up a ridiculous story to get out of spending time with her. She imagined that Eddie was a friend who had been briefed to ring Jed and give him the perfect excuse to do a disappearing act. She felt annoyed and rather hurt that he had felt the need to go to all those lengths to avoid her but was determined to forget all about him. OK, he was attractive, but clearly a total heel, an uppcr class one at that. He was probably born with a silver spoon in his mouth. She had a vague feeling that Milly was well bred, so Jed must be too. He was not worth wasting any more time on and she realised she had spent too long trying to work out what she had done wrong. Instead, she decided to be vague, bright and breezy if questioned by Jack about him. She certainly was too proud to reveal how she really felt.

'So, did you enjoy yourself on Saturday? You seemed to hit it off with Jed,' commented Jack.

'Yeah, it was good. I thought it was probably best to separate Jed and Cassie on balance, don't you think?'

'Yeah. Cassie did come on a bit strong, didn't she? Poor Milly was looking really flustered. So, are you seeing Jed again?' Jack casually threw this into the conversation, presumably having been well briefed by Milly. Imogen wondered what the etiquette was about criticising your boss's brother-in-law and decided to be economical with the truth. She didn't want Milly feeling that she should make Jed apologise to her, as she would be obliged to see him again and that would be too much to bear. She just wanted to forget about the whole unfortunate incident.

'Well, I'm not sure really. He seemed alright though. Quite good with Cassie. She was on fine form, wasn't she?'

Jack gave her a strange look. 'You could say that I suppose if fine form is code for overbearing and antagonistic. I'm just glad she's Milly's boss and not mine. Anyway, how's the data looking?'

Imogen went on to explain what she had found out so far, feeling pleased that it was the end of the matter. She never wanted to have to think or speak about Jed Cavendish ever again. And if she did, that would be a moment too soon for her.

As Imogen changed for taekwondo, she felt her scar on her lower chest. It could have been so much worse, she was so lucky. She had been terrified and scared of her own shadow for months after it happened. That was why she had decided to take up taekwondo classes to give her more confidence. She had worked her way up to black belt and felt that she would be able to handle herself if attacked again and this did give her more confidence. As she and those with the higher belts went through their rhythmic patterns, the sequence of complex movements they repeated, she began to relax. She enjoyed the discipline of the patterns, but she loved sparring more. At tonight's lesson in her group there were the other black belts, one woman and three men. She was paired with a youngish man, Andy Byrne who she regularly sparred with. She made sure her glasses were in place before she went to grab the lapels of his jacket and took great delight in unbalancing him and flipping him onto his back, in one fluid movement.

'Bloody hell, Imo, you're on fire tonight,' he remarked, wiping his brow and getting uneasily to his feet. 'What's going on?'

Imogen beamed. 'Nothing. You're just too slow. What's wrong with you? Come on let's go again.'

She allowed him time to get to his feet and settle himself and then went in there hard, again sending him crashing onto his back. Thank goodness they had the mats down.

Andy looked bewildered. 'Come on Imo, tell me all about it. Something *is* getting to you...'

Imogen merely shrugged. It was hard to explain. The incident with Jed had unsettled her and she needed to release some stress. But there was something else. From time to time the fears crowded in and she needed reassurance that she could protect herself if ever the need arose. She hadn't expected the first attack and what that had taught her was you had to be prepared. The police thought that it was a result of mistaken identity. She had been wearing her brother's hoodie, casual jeans and heeled boots. In the dim light perhaps, she could have been mistaken for Marcus. He certainly knew an assortment of unsavoury people and there were several who might have had reason to attack him. The culprit, though, had never been found, let alone prosecuted and so for that very reason, she kept training.

Imogen showered and settled down to flick through some research papers and articles when her mother rang.

'Hi darling. Are you still OK to see Marcus at the weekend?'

'Yes. I'll be there of course. What time is visiting?'

'Two to four. You'll pick me up at about half one?'

'Yeah. That'll be fine. I'll see you then.'

There was a pause as her mother seemed to be working herself up to saying something further. 'You know, it's really important that we keep on visiting, keep his morale up. Marcus is really going to need us when he gets out.'

Imogen took in a deep breath. It was always like this. Her mother could never see any wrong in Marcus, yet he was the one currently residing at Her Majesty's Pleasure whilst everyone else picked up the pieces. She recognised her mother's weakness where her brother was concerned, resented it, but then frustratingly found herself making excuses for him too. Marcus could always explain his wayward behaviour, his exclusions from school for drugs and his inability to hold down a job. It was always someone else's fault. He had started using cannabis at first and then the problem had escalated to amphetamine, then cocaine and quite possibly anything he could get his hands on. He was a bright boy and he had managed to get into University to study English but had gone from bad to worse after his first year of wild partying. He had taken a year out to go bumming around Europe and had never gone back to resume his studies. The problem escalated when he came home and tried, unsuccessfully, to find a job. He became depressed, stole from his sister and parents to fund his habit, had no direction and then ended up running up cocaine debts which he had no way of repaying. The local dealers sent in their heavies and followed him demanding money, only to find that it was his sister they had stabbed instead. She had borrowed Marcus's hoodie having forgotten her coat and had been cut, with a long gash just under her collarbone, before her assailants realised that they had got the wrong person. Of course, Marcus had been tearful and apologetic, but clearly not enough to change his behaviour, despite stating that this was the shock he needed to make the necessary changes to his life. He was found to be in possession of cocaine soon afterwards and due to the quantity, was imprisoned for suspected dealing. It had broken her parents' hearts. Suddenly, his behaviour wasn't just about him anymore, it had affected other people. She loved him, but she had little faith that he would change his ways.

Imogen decided on a diplomatic approach. 'I know mum. It's just he'll be out in no time and then what?'

There was a slight pause. 'Then, we'll just have to rally round and support him even more. All of us.'

But that was the thing. Imogen didn't know if that would be enough.

Chapter 5

Jed spent the morning at Lydia Fox's yard. After the ride on High Society at Uttoxeter, he decided to take her up on her offer to come down and ride out for her. He certainly needed taking out of himself after the last few days. He had telephoned Eddie's mother after he left the hospital to pass on the doctor's prognosis and was besieged by questions from the O'Neill family. He spoke to Eddie's mother, father and sister, in turn. His mother was on her way over and he had promised to keep in touch. Questions swirled round and round in his mind. The terrible realisation of what Eddie was up to kept intruding into his consciousness and he needed time to process everything. The thought that Eddie might not survive gnawed away at him. Again, he wished that he had just passed the message on and remained ignorant of what Eddie had or hadn't done. Although, logically, he knew he wasn't to blame for what had happened to Eddie, he still found it hard to shake off the feelings of guilt.

Lydia's yard was twenty or so miles outside York in a lovely rural village not far from Walton. She lived in a small cottage and had a yard of about twelve or so horses and some grazing. She shared some of the facilities with two adjoining trainers. These were an all-weather gallop and a field with several hurdle fences arranged in a circle and a ménage where Lydia schooled her horses. Lydia told him that she had previously competed as a show jumper and was keen to use this expertise in training racehorses. Lydia seemed an optimistic type of a person, very down to earth and keen to make an impact in the racing world.

Lydia showed Jed the horses with typical enthusiasm.

36

'This is Ears, also known as a Major Tom,' she pointed out a fine bay horse. 'He had a really good run at Wetherby, it was rather a surprise actually. Let's hope he gets a win soon.' She stroked the horse's ears. 'He loves having his ears pulled, hence the stable name. And there's Roman Holiday and High Society, who you rode, but I'd like you to ride Ragamuffin. It's his first outing tomorrow, so you may as well try him out. 'She pointed to a bright chestnut with a white blaze and three white socks. Lydia fed the horse a polo. 'I'd like your opinion about him.'

'Fine. No problem. It's a nice place you've got here. Very well kept and tidy.' The yard, though small by most standards, was neat and well organised. In fact, it was one of the tidiest yards he had ever seen. He counted about seven horses and a couple of other staff, but he suspected that Lydia probably worked harder than anyone.

'Yeah, I am hoping to expand but it's quite hard to make a name for yourself in racing.' Lydia sighed and ran her fingers through her hair. 'It doesn't help that I'm female, but also the racing world is something of a closed shop. If you don't have family connections, it can be very hard to get established. Even though I have a horsey background, it isn't in racing, so I'm viewed with suspicion it seems. The worlds of racing and show jumping don't seem to mix that well.' She looked momentarily thoughtful and then shrugged her shoulders.

'Hey, I meant to say, terrible news about Eddie O'Neill. I don't know him as well as you do, but he seems like a good guy. I must send him a 'Get Well' card or something. Awful to think that he's ridden loads of horses in one of the most dangerous sports known to man or woman and then has a severe injury driving in a bloody car!'

Jed nodded, emotion nearly choking him. 'Yes. He's in a bad way. The doctors have put him in a medically induced coma in the hope that he'll recover. I can hardly believe it.'

Lydia touched his arm.

37

Jed gave her a sidelong look. The need to confide in someone about his suspicions was quite overpowering.

'Lydia, did you ever hear anything about Eddie?'

Lydia looked at him in confusion. 'Like what?'

Jed considered continuing, but decided it was just too risky. The racing world was very insular and supposing he was wrong? Asking questions was bound to cause speculation and he just couldn't do that to Eddie. He could ruin the career of a friend by raising doubts about his integrity, when for all he knew there might be a simple explanation for what had happened. If he was going to do anything to find out what was going on, then he had to do it alone or with the help of someone outside the world of racing, he decided.

He grinned at Lydia. 'Oh, he seemed to be arguing with Gary McKay after High Society's race. I suppose Gary had good reason to be annoyed with Eddie for taking his job without beating him fair and square too.'

Lydia shrugged. 'Well, that was before my time, so I'd be surprised if Gary was still annoyed. Perhaps, he thought Eddie cut him up or something?'

Jed nodded. 'Yeah, of course.' Trust Lydia to come up with a sensible explanation. He leapt into Ragamuffin's saddle.

'Come on let's find out what you're made of boy.'

Ragamuffin proved a rather thrilling ride. Lydia had outlined her ambitions for him which included some of the classier races. He was delighted when she said she'd be offering Ragamuffin's and other rides to him, though he did privately wonder about how many she would have, especially given the size of the yard. As he chatted, having untacked Ragamuffin, he noticed that she had about four or five empty stables and hoped that she would be filling them shortly. Perhaps, she was right and female trainers did have a harder time than their male counterparts? Still, she seemed to know what she was doing. He felt it was only a matter of time before owners noticed this too. Jed thanked her and drove home, feeling more upbeat. He found he had several voicemails from his agent, Lawrence Kent. His familiar Yorkshire tones cheered him, especially when he realised he was being offered a lot of rides, then it came to him that some of them were probably due to Eddie's accident and instantly felt guilty all over again. So much so, he rang Eddie's mother, who was now by her son's bedside.

'How are things, Mrs O'Neill?'

'Call me Bernadette. Well, Eddie is still in a coma, but Dr French is amazing, so he is. He's explained it all to me and God willing, he'll pull through. Dr French says it's incredible what the human body can do. We just must have faith. I'm just pleased that Eddie has such good friends. One has just left, grand chap, he was.'

'Great.' Jed wondered who had visited. 'Eddie is very popular and well liked.'

There was a pause which sounded suspiciously like Bernadette was sobbing. Jed wondered what on earth he could say that might make her feel better. It must have been incredibly hard travelling to visit your son who was in a coma. He remembered how anguished he had felt when he saw Eddie with all those bloody tubes and machines keeping him alive.

'Look, are you OK? Jockeys are tough creatures and Eddie is tougher than most and very fit. I'm sure that will help.'

Bernadette sniffed. 'I'm sure you're right. It's just such a shock. And he's normally such a safe driver, I can't think how it happened. Perhaps, there was another car involved, we don't know. And the police have been, they said they'll be wanting to talk to you.'

'OK, that's fine. Keep in touch.' Jed said his goodbyes and wondered why on the earth the police wanted to speak to him. It was probably just a routine procedure following a serious accident. After all, he was the last one to have had contact with him and of course the police would have Eddie's mobile and realise that he had contacted him before the accident. He wondered if they had any ideas about who had called him at Uttoxeter. *Twelve in the sixth.* Everything seemed to come back to that message, the message he had forgotten to pass onto Eddie. Uncomfortable thoughts nagged at his brain. What if he hadn't picked up Eddie's phone, what if Eddie hadn't chosen that moment to go and relieve himself? Images swirled round and round. One thing was clear, he had to try and find out who was behind the scam as he was partly responsible for the situation Eddie was in. He was increasingly convinced that the accident was some sort of payback for not following instructions. And what if Eddie didn't pull through? It didn't bear thinking about.

He was at Wetherby the next day and the whole of the changing room seemed oppressive and gloomy without Eddie's cheery presence. The lads had organised a whip round and sent flowers to the hospital. Jed remembered what Mrs O'Neill had said about visitors and wondered who had been and asked the lads.

'Well, I would have been, but I haven't had a moment,' explained Tristan Davies. 'Which ward is it again?' Jed explained and asked some of the others. It seemed that everyone had thought about Eddie and several had intended to visit, but no-one actually had. It must have been some other guys who weren't here, Jed decided, or friends who weren't jockeys. Perhaps, it was someone from the gym?

'Was Eddie OK, did he seem alright generally?' Jed asked Tristan, a popular chap who along with his friend Charlie Durrant were amongst the most successful jockeys in the north.

'Seemed as right as rain, usual weight issues, of course. Come to think of it, he did seem to be struggling more than usual, but that's pretty much par for the course, an occupational hazard, you might say. Why, what are you thinking?'

'Well, he did have that argument with Gary.'

Tristan shrugged. 'Gary would argue with his own shadow sometimes.' He nodded to the man in the corner who was scowling and silent, avoiding the usual jocular banter. 'Look at him. He's a miserable sod at the best of times. Unless you know something you're not telling me...'

Jed really wanted to confide in someone, to explain what he had heard when he picked up the Eddie's phone, but he couldn't do it, not here in the weighing room of all places when all the lads were about.

'No, I don't know anything.' The lie tripped easily off Jed's lips. 'I just miss the old bugger.'

Tristan punched his arm. 'We all do, mate. Look, just think of the injuries we've all had, some worse than others. It's amazing how the body can heal itself. He's in the best place. Strange though...' Tristan ran his fingers through his blond hair. 'I went to Cheltenham with him and he was driving so bloody slowly, he really was. A real 'steady Eddie' he was, almost like a learner driver. I remember teasing him relentlessly to put his bloody toe down.' Tristan grinned at the memory. 'I just can't see him having an accident. Perhaps, he nodded off or another car hit him?'

Jed took this in. He had often drove Eddie to the races as he had a swish Audi and enjoyed driving, but he was aware of Eddie's steady reputation.

'I know what you mean, mate.'

Jed had a third place in the first race, ran down the field in two others and amazingly was placed fourth on Lydia's Ragamuffin on the horse's first outing. Then it was back down to earth in the sixth, when his horse fell two from home and he ended up curling into a ball and narrowly avoiding being trampled on by the remainder of the field. As he was checked over by the St John's ambulance and driven back to the changing room, he reflected on life's ups and downs. He also wondered how a man for whom the phrase 'steady Eddie' could have been coined, had been involved in such a serious car accident, if indeed it was an accident. His heart contracted at the thought of other possibilities.

Chapter 6

Hull Prison was a depressing place at the best of times, but as they waited to see Marcus, it seemed greyer and more austere than usual. The skies were full of marbled clouds, giving little hope of the rain clearing and the wind blowing off the grey river Humber, added to the pervading gloomy atmosphere. The bulk of the prison was Victorian with various modern extensions and as they waited to have their paperwork checked, Imogen felt that the stench of human misery was imbued in every brick and every closed door. The staff began the process of unlocking a wide variety of doors and gates as they walked the short distance to an area where they were searched. The rules were strict to avoid illicit items or weapons being brought in for the prisoners. A clutch of young women with children and babies were being stopped from taking their pushchairs in. They were restricted to a child's bib, bottle and little else, as there were just too many places to hide contraband, such as drugs or weapons. A blonde woman, chewing gum and clutching a crying baby, uttered profanities as the staff explained this to her. She shook her head, spat out her gum and carried the baby on her hip, having been asked to leave her changing bag outside. She bit back at the prison officer with an angry retort as he patiently explained the rules. Imogen and her mother avoided the woman's eye, it didn't do to be seen staring. These were desperate people who wouldn't think twice about taking their anger out on other visitors.

They were shown into a small room where there were several tables and chairs and a variety of expectant prisoners. At the far end, prison officers surveyed them from some sort of platform. Marcus was waiting for them. He was wearing an incongruous orange bib, as though he was about to launch into a game of netball. He grinned at them cheerily enough but looked tired and a little thinner in the face.

'Good to see you both,' he said. 'How are you sis? How's dad?'

Mum smiled. 'Oh, dad's fine, just a bit too busy to come today.' Imogen wondered how long they would keep up the pretence. The fact was that their father was too disappointed, too angry and too damned humiliated to visit his son in prison. Surely, Marcus knew that too? Imogen felt the need to fill the awkward silence.

'I'm fine, beavering away at theUniversity, you know… How about you?'

'Well, I'm OK all things considered. I just want to get out and get settled, you know…'

Mrs James smiled and touched his hand. 'We know. Had any thoughts about what you might do for a job when you leave?'

'Well, the fact is,' Marcus lowered his voice. 'I've been having a bit of luck on the gee gees. Not that we can bet, of course, but we do trade cigs, mags, privileges, and some of the lads have taught me stuff, you know, a bit about betting systems. So, I wondered about working for a bookie or something like that when I come out.'

A light died somewhere in Mrs James's eyes at the mention of bookmakers and racehorses. Imogen found herself thinking about Jed Cavendish. Although it was an unwelcome thought, at least it might provide much needed fodder for their rather stilted conversation.

'Oh, my boss invited me to a meal recently and I met that jockey, Jed Cavendish, talking of jockeys.'

Marcus looked interested. 'Oh. I think he was quite a good amateur. Did you get any useful tips?'

'No. I'm not really into racing.' Or jockeys come to mention it, she thought, feeling suddenly rather bleak.

The conversation appeared to be sticking and Imogen found herself looking round at the other inmates and their visitors as their mother quizzed Marcus about his general health. She spotted the gum chewing blonde smiling at a thick set man with a shaved head and lots of tattoos. The woman was quite pretty when she wasn't scowling and swearing. Then her eyes were drawn to the next table, to a man probably in his fifties, who looked completely unlike the other inmates. He looked refined and professional, like a doctor or a solicitor. His greying hair was well cut, and he had fine patrician features. He was talking to two young men in baseball caps. His sons, she presumed. She found herself wondering what crime this man had committed. The tables were quite close together and the young men sat far back from the table, with their legs stretched out ahead of them. One of the lads passed a mars bar to the older man, who pocketed it quickly. She supposed it was hard to get chocolate in the prison. She could hear snatches of their conversation and was sure that they could hear what they were talking about. So much for privacy.

There was a pause. 'Imogen's got some ideas what you might want to do when you get out, haven't you Imogen...'

Imogen's heart sank. 'Yes, I had wondered if you should just finish off your degree. That was all and of course, I keep looking out for jobs at the University but there's not been too much lately, what with cutbacks and so on. Perhaps dad has some ideas?'

Surely their father could find him something at the engineering company where he had worked for thirty years, Imogen thought rather crossly? Why was it always up to her to clean up after Marcus's messes? But again, there was the seemingly insurmountable problem of a drugs conviction to deal with. Marcus was frowning at both suggestions.

Mrs James smiled bravely. 'Well, I'm sure something will turn up, darling. You were always such a bright boy. Perhaps, you could go into business if you don't go back to University, do something entrepreneurial. You ought to think about it.' Imogen thought that her mother had been watching too much 'Dragon's Den' again and swooning over 'that nice Peter Jones'.

Marcus sniffed. 'Yeah. That's what I was thinking with the betting malarkey. With this system, I would have won and been quids in. It turns out I've a bit of a talent for it, with the help of a bit of inside info. I would have won even more if it wasn't for the sixth race at Uttoxeter...' He tailed off, his irritation plain.

Mrs James looked confused. 'What did you say, Uttoxeter? It sounds like a disease, or something.'

Marcus laughed. 'No, mum, it's a racecourse.'

Imogen thought the place sounded rather familiar, then remembered that Jed had talked about racing there.

Mrs James sniffed and turned the conversation to safer waters like football, what the neighbours were up to, the garden, holidays and checked on Marcus's eating habits.

'What's the food like?' she asked, as though it was a hotel rather than a prison.

Marcus shrugged. 'So, so...'

Imogen wondered about Marcus's betting comments. What on earth Marcus was getting into? Still, she did not want to think about bloody race meetings after the other evening. She found her attention wandering off again, to the group assembled at the other table. I bet that guy is inside for fraud, she found herself thinking, or some crime that required intelligence. Certainly, nothing that involved muscle. Her mother nudged her as the conversation had once again become rather stilted.

'I suppose you'll be on Probation when you get out?' Imogen found herself asking. She wondered what Marcus was learning inside and whether all those studies she'd read about, that prisons only increased the likelihood of an inmate returning to a life of crime due to their associates sharing professional secrets and skills, were accurate. The thought of Marcus surviving without the support of such an organisation as Probation was very worrying indeed.

'Yeah. They'll keep me on the straight and narrow, sis. Probably, have some careers advice too.'

Mrs James brightened. 'Yes. I'm sure they will dear, I'm sure they will.'

Having dropped her mother off, promising to redouble her efforts to look out for jobs for Marcus, Imogen picked up her post and made herself a sandwich as she flicked through it. There were several bills and a postcard. She flicked over the postcard with its bright seascape scene and jolted as she recognised the slanted, small handwriting. Sam. She read his words eagerly.

Hi babe. Having a great time travelling around Bali. It is a heavenly place, so much to see and do. How is the research going? Hope you are well and that you enjoyed your summer. Sam x

Imogen read and reread the card looking for any clues in the text as to how he was feeling about her or when he would be back in the UK. But there was nothing. Disappointment filled her mouth, a sour, bitter taste. It was crystal clear that she had been well and truly relegated from his girlfriend to a complete nobody. It was so impersonal it could have been written to a maiden aunt, she decided.

47

She had been in a relationship with Sam for three years for God's sake and everything had seemed to be going swimmingly. Then he had announced that he 'felt trapped' and wanted to travel round the world whilst he was still young. He politely suggested that they should remain friends as he couldn't expect her to 'wait for him.' Imogen had been devastated but had declared that 'too right' she wasn't bloody well waiting for him. He could piss right off.

Unhappily, she realised he had done just that having clearly been planning his escape for many more months than he had let on. She had wanted to show him what he was missing with wild partying, an image change, weight loss, especially the obstinate ten pounds or so that she couldn't quite shift, but he had shipped out with indecent haste, so fast that he never got to see her carefully constructed revenge. Damn him. Bloody Sam and now after the incident with Jed, she decided enough was enough. Someone making up an obvious lie just to get away from her, that was truly an all time low. She peered in the mirror, pulled off her glasses and released her hair from its tight bun. What was the phrase that Jack used when thinking about different ways of looking at problems? If you do what you always do, then you'll get what you usually get. He had meant to apply this to research, but it could certainly help in her present situation. She had to break out of this negative cycle somehow. Perhaps, it was time for a drastic change of image?

Chapter 7

Having checked on Eddie's condition, there was no change, Jed made his way to Market Rasen races. He was riding in four of the races and was beginning to feel like a real pro, just like the other lads. He was riding one for Kieron McLoughlin who Eddie usually rode for, one for Lydia Fox and one for Miles Jamieson. Charlie Durrant was Miles's stable jockey, but as he had two runners, Jed was offered the ride on the least fancied horse. That was fine with him. Then he had a ride for a small trainer, Niall Curley. There was a great deal of excitement because the whole meeting was being televised for the new programme 'Racing Days' and there was much speculation about who might win first and be interviewed by the delectable Felicity Hill. Even Tristan Davies, who was usually poring over the Racing Post, looked up and joined in the speculation about who would get the honour first. However, Tristan was less than impressed.

'I don't know what all the fuss is about. Bet she's as dull as ditch water under all that fake tan and stuff. Bring back Penny Morris, is what I say. At least she knew the business inside out, unlike the new girl.' There were many nods and comments of agreement. Penny had been unceremoniously dumped to make way for the new glamorous presenter. 'Felicity treats the show like a bloody fashion shoot, you know.'

Jed nodded. He liked Penny and thought she had been treated appallingly. From what he had seen of Felicity, he was deeply mistrustful about her.

'Still, I wouldn't mind being interviewed by her. She usually takes the top jocks out for a celebratory drink, or at least she did with Eddie,' piped up Jake Horton, with ill-disguised anticipation.

'Yeah and look what happened to him,' complained Tristan. 'How is the old boy, by the way? I hope he liked the flowers we sent him.'

'Still in a coma, so I doubt it. His mother is over here now, so at least she'll appreciate them. They hope he'll make a full recovery, but you can never tell.'

There was a hushed silence as everyone contemplated the severity of his injuries which wouldn't have surprised them in their sport, but from a car crash, well it didn't bear thinking about.

'Bags I get the first interview with Felicity,' quipped Gavin Shearing, a young conditional. 'My horse, Be My Guest, will walk it.'

'Nah, not a chance,' replied Gary McKay, the older, dour jockey. 'You useless bastards are gonna be outclassed by my horse, Avanti. You wait, that Felicity Hill is gonna be eating out of my hand.'

There was a volley of comments across the weighing room after that, which put Gary firmly in his place. As usual, Gary McKay put a dampener on the jocular atmosphere. Gary merely sneered at the comments and turned away, the miserable sod. Everyone ignored him, and Jed was pleased to find that normal weighing room banter was resumed after a few minutes.

As it turned out, Jed was the jockey to claim the prize first, having had a win on Medici, Kieron McLoughlin's horse, in the first race. He had ridden a good finish to beat the horse ridden by Tristan Davies by about half a length. Kieron seemed pleased and clapped him on the back. Jed noticed that he had engaged a handful of less well-known jockeys to ride his horses in Eddie's absence, probably trying them all out. He hoped that Kieron thought he had ridden well and wondered if he'd get some more rides, then berated himself at the thought. He was delighted to notice that Gary McKay's horse trailed in last. Jed rode into the winner's enclosure to great applause and dismounted when he heard a soft voice behind him. He turned to find Felicity flanked by two TV cameras, clutching a fluffy microphone.

'Jed. Can we have a word with the winning jockey?' she pouted, slipped her arm through his and leaned into him. She was tall, slight and her blonde curls were pinned up into a messy up do. She was also an unlikely shade of mahogany and was wearing a fitted tight pink skirt which finished mid-thigh, a matching jacket with a low-cut top that skimmed her breasts. Jed found he was almost asphyxiated by her heavy perfume. Her blue eyes twinkled, and Jed's first thought was that she could have been very pretty if it wasn't for the overblown makeup. He fought the urge to rub the fake tan off her skin to reveal the white skin underneath. She reminded him of a little girl who had been playing around with her mother's makeup, except that her eyes were as sharp as tacks.

'Sure,' he replied. Felicity grinned and licked her lips.

'Cool,' she referred to her notes. 'So, Jed Cavendish, you rode really hard at the end of that race to win.' Felicity pouted, pushing her chest out in a faintly suggestive manner. 'Is this your first winner of the season?'

'Yes.' There was a pause and Jed realised she was struggling what to ask next, so ever the gentleman he decided to help her out. 'Actually, it's my first winner as a professional and I'm delighted to have ridden a winner for Kieron McLoughlin.' He noticed Felicity baulk slightly at Kieron's name and the obvious link to Eddie O'Neill.

Felicity's smile faltered. 'Really? So, you're quite new to race riding? What did you do before becoming a jockey?'

'Well, I was an amateur jockey.' There was an awkward pause whilst Felicity recovered herself and moved swiftly on.

'Great. Brilliant. So, you've picked up the ride because Kieron McLoughlin's regular jockey, Eddie O'Neill, is in hospital, that's right isn't it?'

'Yes. He was involved in a car accident and is badly injured.'

Felicity assumed a suitably sombre expression.

'Well, we wish him all the best and hope he'll be back riding soon. I suppose you might pick up some more of his rides whilst he's out of action?'

Jed was momentarily nonplussed.

'Well, that's up to Kieron to decide, but I'd just like to wish Eddie a speedy recovery, that's all.'

Felicity nodded looking rather awkward.

'So, I think you've got some other rides here today? How do you think you'll do?'

Jed shrugged. 'I have a one for Lydia Fox and another for Miles Jamieson. Lydia prepares and schools her horses carefully and I think her horses could do well. She's definitely an up and coming trainer.' No harm in trying to do Lydia a bit of good, he decided, thinking back to her half empty stables.

Felicity looked at her notes. 'Yes, yes of course, well prepared and schooled, wonderful.' She recovered herself and read a question off her sheet. 'This race was a two- mile handicap, which Medici won fairly easily in the end, what other plans does Kieron have for the horse?'

Jed wanted to help Felicity out, but it was not anything that he and Kieran has discussed.

'I'm not sure. You'll have to ask him, but he showed good form today and had lots more to give, I'd say. There's lots of options for him, to be honest.'

Felicity grinned at the camera. 'Great. Well, congratulations on your win, Jed. I hope there will be many more. Jed Cavendish, ladies and gentlemen, the winning jockey.'

She gave him a grateful look before disappearing to try and find Kieron He suspected that she might try and have a quick word with Lydia too. He wondered what on earth she would make of Felicity, as they were polar opposites, the wholesome trainer and ex-glamour model. As Jed unsaddled Medici and went back to the weighing room, he wondered who on earth Felicity knew to have landed such a top job, because it was obvious that she had no aptitude whatsoever for the position and would never have been given such a role on her own merit. He also wondered about her relationship with Eddie. Then he pictured him lying in his hospital bed and felt a wave of misery wash over him. Eddie, what the hell are you caught up in?

The rest of the afternoon was something of a mixed bag. Lydia's horse ran down the field and showed little promise, Miles Jamieson's horse put in a good effort to finish fourth behind his other horse ridden by Charlie Durrant, but Niall Curley's horse had to be pulled up as he rattled the fourth fence and came up lame. Jed felt the uneven gait and the horse's pull to the side so reined him to a halt. Jed dismounted and felt his horse's off fore which would surely be radiating with the tell-tale heat of a soft tissue injury come the morning. Yet now there was no sign of any abrasion or injury. He discussed the lameness with the trainer and the worried looking owners. The vet was called upon to pronounce on his injury. Still, overall, he'd had a good win and a fourth place, so he left the races in good spirits.

Back at his cottage he was just settling down to eat a salad and a well-deserved glass of wine and was mulling over the events of the day, when two detectives arrived. DI Roberts was stocky, dark haired with the look of a rugby player, if his broken nose was anything to go by. His colleague DC Cooper was younger, sandy haired man with a more blokey air about him. Both were wearing plain clothes and looked serious. After some pleasantries, they began.

'So, Mr Cavendish can you tell us how Eddie O'Neill seemed when you last saw him?'

'Fine, his usual self. I was riding at Uttoxeter and so was he.'

DI Roberts nodded. 'Anything different about him, unusual?'

'No, he seemed his usual self. But there was something. I answered his phone when he was in the loo. It was a bit strange, but it was just before the thirty minute cut off point where we have to switch our mobiles off.' DI Roberts and DS Cooper looked at him blankly. 'You know, the BHA has a rule whereby the jockeys all have to switch off their phones thirty minutes before the start of the first race, until after the last race. I suppose it's about protecting the integrity of racing,' Jed added.

DI Roberts nodded. 'So, if this was before the thirty minute cut off point, why did you think the call was strange?'

'It was more what the caller said. You see I meant to turn it off but ended up speaking to whoever was ringing. He just said *twelve in the sixth.*'

'What did you think that meant?'

Jed looked from one to the other. He had a pretty good idea, but he wasn't going to do all the work for them. He also didn't want to sully Eddie's name unnecessarily.

'No idea. I forgot to pass the information on because it seemed like a crank call. When Eddie came back, we were talking about something else.'

DI Roberts pursed his lips. 'So, Eddie didn't know about the message, if it was a message?'

DC Cooper wrote down *twelve in the sixth,* in a curled, stylish hand.

'No.

'Did Eddie contact you afterwards, at all?' The question was casual, but DI Robert's eyes were sharp.

'Yes. I went to my sister's place for a meal and ended up in the pub. I had to dash off because Eddie rang me. He sounded distressed and incoherent and he said he was at the gym, so I went there to meet him, but he never showed up. I was going to pop by his house when I came across his car and the crash. Have you any idea how it happened? Was there any other car involved?'

The two men exchanged a look.

DI Roberts spoke. 'We are pursuing several lines of inquiry at the moment, sir. Were you aware whether or not Eddie was on any medication?'

'No, not really except those tablets he was taking. He was struggling to make the weights and seemed to be popping the things like no tomorrow and having saunas. They were just all natural, according to him, nothing sinister,' Jed added as an after thought. He didn't want to make things any worse for Eddie. He knew that some diuretics were banned by the BHA and could lead to an investigation.

DI Roberts nodded. 'Well, that is something that we're looking at. Possibly, he was so dehydrated that he could have simply passed out whilst he was driving. Blackouts are not unusual in such cases.' DI Roberts fiddled with a loose piece of paper from his pocketbook, appeared to unfold it, studied it and then placed it under his book. 'Yes, that could be one explanation for the accident.'

Jed sighed. He was surprised that natural tablets were being blamed for the crash.

'Really, I've no idea they were that effective. He said they contained dandelion, ginger and parsley, so they can't have been. Poor Eddie. Do you think he'll make it?'

'He's in good hands, so he's in with a fighting chance. Is there anything else you can think of? Was Eddie in any trouble, did he tell you why he wanted to meet you, for example?'

'No, I could barely understand him actually. After the accident I received this text, though. Look.'

He fished in his pocket for his mobile and showed them the text.

DC Cooper copied it carefully into his notebook.

'What do you think he might have meant?' DI Roberts frowned. *'I've really ballsed things up…'*

'I've no idea.'

'Could he have been referring to him having taken an overdose, do you think?'

Jed nearly laughed. 'What an overdose of herbal tablets? I don't think so, it doesn't make any sense. He wasn't racing for a couple of days so why would he bother to take more tablets after the race? Surely, he'd wait until the next race meeting? A jockey can lose four to five pounds on race day with a sauna or jogging wearing excess clothing, but there would be no point after the races, you'd only take them before you weighed in.'

'Maybe he'd overdone the tablets the previous day,' suggested DC Cooper.

Jed suddenly thought of something. 'By the way, did you find his phone?'

'Yes, but it was damaged in the crash and therefore we are having to use telephone records which have limited information.' DI Roberts looked thoughtful.

'Right.' That would mean they would have details of calls but not of text messages or of the names of callers. Not so useful as they wouldn't be able to trace the person who had rung Eddie with that strange message. *Twelve in the Sixth.* Jed tried to imagine what the force of the crash must have been like to damage a phone to that extent. It didn't bear thinking about.

DI Roberts nodded gravely and stirred. 'Can you think of anyone who would want to harm Eddie?'

Jed shook his head. 'No, he is really popular, everyone's favourite Irishman. I don't think Gary McKay liked being beaten by Eddie's mount and the two had a bit of a row, but Gary can be a bit volatile really.'

'Enough to harm Mr O'Neill, would you say?'

Jed thought about this seriously. 'No. I can't see it myself.'

DI Roberts pursed his lips.

'Hmm. Indeed. Well Sir, if you think about anything else then do give me us a call.'

'And if you have any racing tips, too,' quipped his colleague.

As he saw them out, Jed thought that the only tip he could give them was to try harder. He was pretty sure that Eddie wouldn't have taken an overdose of tablets and he was not at all sure that the police would look any further than the end of their noses. They seemed satisfied with a straightforward explanation, but Jed was far from convinced. How could a couple of tablets have caused him to blackout? What the hell was in the things? It seemed ridiculous. Jockeys had saunas on race days, a few tried other things like sucking on ice cubes to reduce fluid intake or even 'flipping' or making themselves sick, to lose a few pounds to make the weights, but he had never heard of someone doing this after the race. There was nothing for it, he was going to have to look into the matter himself. He began to clear up and it was then he noticed the folded piece of paper on the floor near where the inspector had sat. He unfolded it and realised that it was the blood test results for Eddie. He peered at the paper and read levels for *serum osmolality, blood urea nitrogen* and *hemocrit* with a row of figures next to them and realised he had absolutely no idea what these figures meant. It might as well be a foreign language. He needed someone with specialist knowledge to assist him. Milly might know someone working at the University, perhaps even Jack? Then he realised that Jack was more of a statistician and probably wouldn't be able to interpret these results. Then it came to him. He realised he knew just the person to help him and reached for his phone. He had an awful lot of explaining to do.

Chapter 8

Imogen found that the contact lenses had been something of revelation. She soon mastered the art of putting them in and removing them by making a pinching movement with her forefinger and thumb. She felt much freer without her black framed spectacles and had to admit that she looked pretty good. She would still wear her glasses when her eyes were sore or when she needed a touch of gravitas, like when taking a seminar or something. But the hair, which she had been persuaded by her stylist to have cut into a chin length, choppy bob, was even better. It showed off her bone structure and she felt lighter and more alive somehow. She caught sight of herself reflected in shop windows and felt a jolt of surprise at the difference such minor changes could make. The reaction from friends had been one of delight, whereas Jack had stared at her in amazement when she came into work on Monday morning.

Imogen had caught his look and mistaken it.

'I know, it is a drastic change, but it will grow back...' she added.

Jack closed his mouth and peered at the layers. 'Well, I bloody well hope not. You look so different, in a good way, naturally. Well done.'

Imogen recognised this as praise indeed and felt her heart lift. She had been so low about Sam. If he could disappear and enjoy himself without so much as a backward glance in her direction, then so could she. She'd also joined the University gym and hoped to get a little fitter and lose some weight. She wanted to tone up her body and feel better about herself. Although, she was a regular at taekwondo, there was still room for improvement in terms of fitness and weight. She had reread Sam's postcard, winced at its impersonal tone and tossed it in the bin. She had also arranged to go out with friends at the weekend. She was absolutely done with feeling sorry for herself. Enough was enough.

Jack soon began discussing some statistics with her and asking her opinion about them, so it was business as usual. When she had a minute, she intended to look up the vacancies on the internal website at the University. She had promised her mother that she would look for a job for Marcus, but the reality of his prison sentence for drug dealing was going to be rather hard to overlook, she suspected. She had felt deflated by her visit to the prison. The place always depressed her and although she felt some sympathy for Marcus, it faded when she realised that he just did not have the right attitude for proper rehabilitation back into normal society. Wasn't he supposed to be remorseful and determined to make a fresh start? Instead, he was arrogant and had worried her mother by being so enthusiastic about betting, even hinting that it was something he was thinking of taking up as a career. Her mother had been uncharacteristically quiet on the journey back home, only brightening when Imogen had suggested that together with the family's help and good professional support, she was sure things would improve for Marcus. Imogen had dropped her mother off home with a very heavy heart. Marcus's release date was in about three months, if everything went according to plan and although they would all be pleased, it would mean that the dreadful worries about him would begin again.

Imogen was just flicking through the University's jobs page and discarding all the academic posts, wondering if Marcus would be able to manage a porter's job, when Amanda, the Department's business support assistant appeared with an expectant expression on her face. She was not alone, but at first Imogen could not see who was with her due to Amanda's large girth blocking the doorway and obscuring the visitor.

'Someone to see you,' she said. At first, Imogen had the strangest thought that it might be Sam and was just beginning to try to compose herself when Amanda stepped aside, and she saw who it was. Jed. He looked rather handsome, his dark hair falling over one eye and clearly Amanda was impressed, so much so, she was almost swooning. Imogen noticed that he was also bearing a large bouquet of flowers, a bottle of wine and a sheepish expression.

'Mr Cavendish,' announced Amanda, hovering.

'Thanks, Amanda.' Imogen showed him into her office and promptly closed the door, aware of Amanda's acute disappointment at being denied the opportunity to eavesdrop. She surveyed her guest, annoyance surging through her.

'God. I never expected to see you again. You really do have a nerve turning up here. I must admit I've never had someone get their friend to ring up and feign illness to be relieved of my company. That was definitely a first. You certainly know how to make as girl feel like shit.'

Jed looked contrite. 'I know, I know, except that it was all true and if you allow me to take you out for lunch and explain, you'll realise that too. Besides, I need your help.'

'What about?'

Jed hesitated. 'Well, I need information about the side effects of drugs, actually.' He advanced towards her and she caught the delightful scent of lilies from the impressive bouquet he was carrying. He looked mournful. 'Please, just hear me out.'

Despite her intention to ask him to leave, she found herself intrigued. Besides, it was lunch time and she had to eat after all. She

61

was sure he would pick up the tab and the lure of a free lunch was hard to ignore.

She looked at her watch. 'OK. You have thirty minutes.'

They ate at one of the University's cafes after Imogen had found a vase for the flowers.

'You look different, new hairdo suits you.' Jed sat down and surveyed her. Imogen ignored him. She wasn't about to let him off that easily, but she found her spirits lifting anyway.

'OK. So, what happened on Saturday night to make you dash off and why do you need my help? I'm all ears.'

Jed looked around at the crowd of students chatting at their tables and lowered his voice.

'Well, firstly my friend and fellow jockey, Eddie O'Neill is lying in hospital in a coma after a car accident. It was him that called me when I was with you.'

Imogen took this in. So, he had been genuine after all.

'Oh God. I'm sorry. But how do you think I can help?'

'OK. What do you know about natural water tablets? If taken in excess would they be damaging?' He fished in his pocket and showed her a photo of the tablets he had saved.

Imogen looked at the photo. 'Well, they are made by a reputable company. She enlarged the photo in one deft movement. 'It says they contain dandelion, ginger, parsley, black seed and hibiscus. Pretty natural, well-known ingredients.' She sipped her coffee and thought carefully, wondering why he wanted to know.

Jed nodded. 'If taken to excess would those ingredients be harmful or cause dehydration?'

'Not if the correct amounts were taken and it would depend on the concentration and quality of the ingredients, I suppose.'

'And if larger quantities were taken?'

'Well, it would be possible. If used to excess, then they could cause the body to lose vital electrolytes. In the long term, they could cause dehydration and affect the heart eventually, I suppose, but you'd need to take an awful lot of the stuff as these would be less effective than pharmacological grade diuretics.'

Jed nodded. 'OK. What are the effects of dehydration?'

'Confusion, cramps, blackouts in severe cases. Why do you want to know?'

'Because Eddie O'Neill was struggling to make the weights and had taken these water tablets. Diuretics are banned by the BHA, so the theory is that Eddie took these instead of prescribed diuretics as none of the chemicals are on the banned list. He police think that he could have taken too many and this caused him to become dehydrated, black out and crash his car.'

'And you don't believe it?'

'No. He showed be the pack and he'd only taken four from a blister pack. I suppose he could have taken more before, but I think Eddie was involved in race fixing.'

Imogen looked at the hazel eyes and wondered if Jed was quite sane. It seemed quite a leap to her.

'Well, why not let the police do their job, that's what they are there for.' She knew she sounded patronising, as though she was humouring a small child, but it was obvious, wasn't it?

Jed gave a grim smile. 'Look. Let me explain.'

He went on to tell her the whole story. Imogen listened intently. It was a fantastic tale. After several minutes she sat back in her chair and gazed at Jed.

'So, let me get this straight. Because of a bizarre message you took on Eddie's phone, *'twelve in the sixth'*, which you didn't pass on, Eddie wins the race when you think he was supposed to have lost. So, he was 'punished' for not doing what was asked of him. This punishment was made to look like a car accident, so much so, that the police don't seem to be pursuing the case that vigorously. But because of this, you think that Eddie was injured by race fixing criminals who presumably are still at large.'

Jed toyed with his salad and pointed his knife at her. 'You're forgetting the text he sent before the accident which I received later.'

'Right, the one which said, *I've really ballsed things up.'*

Jed nodded. 'Which suggests to me that he was in some sort of trouble.'

Imogen finished her drink. 'Maybe he sent it because he was feeling physically ill and knew he'd taken too many tablets…'

'Hmm. The police thought that too…'

'But you don't agree?'

Jed speared a tomato. 'No, because Eddie was taking the tablets for weight loss in the same way that most jockeys have saunas, go jogging, and the rest of it *before* the race. You do that to make the weight for the weigh in, so why bother taking more tablets after the race? It doesn't make any sense. Jockeys can lose five pounds with all those tricks, but it would be pointless doing it after a race.'

'What weights do you need to ride at?'

'Oh, about ten or eleven stone for jump jockeys.'

Imogen gasped. 'But that's nothing for someone your height.' Privately, she thought they were all bloody mad. 'Anyway, what has any of this got to do with me?'

Jed looked at her steadily. 'Well, I have decided to look into the matter myself. It's the least I can do for Ed, I'm sort of the reason he's in hospital because of not passing on that stupid, bloody message.'

'Yes, but how can I help?'

'Because, you know about drugs, you're very smart and I think you care about justice and the truth, if I'm any judge.' Jed appeared to hesitate and then fished a piece of paper out of his pocket. 'Look. These are his blood test results. I'd be really grateful of you could have a look at them, cast your professional eye over them and see if you think Eddie was dehydrated to that extent. Besides, I need someone who is removed from racing to help me, someone objective, clever, like you. And I want justice for Eddie, to find out who was blackmailing him to do it.'

'How did you get these?'

Jed grinned. 'By fair means, not foul.'

What the hell did that mean? Imogen folded the paper and slipped it into her diary, thinking she would look at them later. She couldn't help think that Jed had a very rosy view of his friend.

'You don't know he was being blackmailed, he may have been paid, for all you know. I hate to break it to you, but he could be really corrupt. Simple really.'

Jed shook his head. 'No, not Eddie. Someone *made* him pull races.'

'And the other thing is if your friend is involved with race fixing and to all intents and purposes getting away with it, then why expose him?'

Jed sighed. 'I suppose it's about doing the right thing. Suppose Eddie dies, and no-one finds out the real reason why and the criminals get away with it. Not to mention the sport that I love being wrecked by the bastards. Besides, I owe it to Eddie.' Imogen noted the real passion in his voice. 'Will you help me? I'll leave you my number, if you want to think about it.'

Imogen took the card put it with the piece of paper Jed had given her. She thought about Marcus and his recent betting revelations. What was it he'd said? Something about the last race at Uttoxeter. She glanced at her watch.

'Look, I've got to dash. Thanks for lunch and the flowers. Bye.' She turned back. 'Listen, where was this race that Eddie was supposed to pull?'

'Uttoxeter. He was riding Happy Days, number twelve in the sixth race at Uttoxeter, the last race. You see it fits, *twelve in the sixth.*' He waited for this to sink in. 'But instead of losing, he won and then was involved in a serious car accident. You see, there's definitely something dodgy going on.'

Imogen glanced at her watch and realised she had to get over to the other side of the campus for a meeting in about three minutes. Lunch had taken twice as long as she'd thought it would. She gathered up her things, her brain spinning. Surely, it had to be a coincidence?

'I'll think about it and let you know...'

With that she turned on her heel, deep in thought.

Chapter 9

Jed called into the hospital after he left the University. Eddie
was still wired up to machines that beeped rhythmically, his room
looked like a florist shop and his mother, Bernadette, was sitting at his
side reading extracts from the Racing Post to him. She was delighted
to meet Jed and shook his hand with enthusiasm.

'Oh, it's a great pleasure to meet you in person. You've been
such a friend to Eddie, so you have. The times he's mentioned you.
I'm so glad he has such good friends. A Scottish chap was here too.'
Mrs O'Neill was small, well preserved with bobbed blonde hair and
penetrating blue eyes, just like Eddie's. Underneath the smiles, her
expression was strained with the effort of putting on a brave face. Jed
wondered who the Scottish chap was, could it be Gary McKay? Surely
not. There were lots of Scottish people in Yorkshire, so he shouldn't
make assumptions.

'That's great. Eddie is very popular with everyone. So, how is
he doing? What do the doctors say?'

Bernadette sighed and patted her hair. 'Well, the doctors are
amazing. They say it's just a question of waiting, that's all.'

Jed pulled up a chair and looked at Eddie's pale face. He had
a few cuts and bruises that were now vivid red and purple as the
bruising came out.

'So, how long is it since you've seen him before now?' Jed
asked.

'Oh, not so long ago. He was back for his cousin's confirmation a few weeks back and had a race at Punchestown.'

'And how did he seem then?'

'Grand. No problem at all.' Bernadette shot him a look. 'Why?'

'Oh, nothing. I just wondered if he was OK, happy, not homesick or worried about something, that's all.'

Bernadette's face softened. 'Well, he might well be homesick, missing us all, he's a terrible home body, but it's what he wanted to do, be the hot shot jockey.' She clutched at Eddie's hand, stifling a sob. 'And then he nearly kills himself in a car. He wasn't even a fast driver, that's the mystery.' Her tears glistened down her cheeks.

'Look. He's in the best place and he's actually survived much worse. Remember that fall at Cheltenham?'

Bernadette dabbed at her eyes. 'You're right, but then sometimes I think has his luck run out, you know? We'll just have to hope and pray…'

Jed noticed the pull-out bed in the corner. What must it be like turning up in England on your own, visiting your son who was in a coma? She must feel so alone not to mention uncomfortable judging by the flimsy look of the bed. He made a sudden decision.

'Bernadette, where are you staying? Here at the hospital?'

She nodded. 'It's the best place. I'm worried he'll wake up and I'll miss him.'

A wild idea came to him. 'Look. Why don't you stay at my house? It's fifteen minutes on foot from here and I've two spare rooms. '

Bernadette smiled. 'I wouldn't want to put you to any trouble. Besides, I can always stay at Eddie's place.'

Jed suddenly had a brainwave. 'Well, if you have the keys to his house, perhaps I could stay there occasionally when I've an early start? I need to be nearer Walton now I'm riding more, and you need to be in York. I can take you to my house in a minute if you like. If you give the nurses a contact number, then they can ring if they need you.' Jed thought he might not actually stay at Eddie's, but it could be useful to look around the place for any clues.

Bernadette nodded. 'Well, that bed is altogether lumpy.' She nodded at the mattress in the corner. 'And it's noisy in here, with patients coming and going in the middle of the night. Are you sure?'

'Completely.'

'Then, I accept. It's so kind of you.' Bernadette smiled broadly. She looked about ten years younger.

'Brilliant. That's settled then.'

Half an hour later, Jed showed Bernadette around his town house and wished he'd had the foresight to tidy up beforehand. Seeing things through her eyes made him feel quite ashamed. The sink was full of dirty pots, his living room was untidy, with papers and plates strewn about and the bathroom floor was littered with towels. Bernadette immediately began washing up and cleaning the surfaces whilst he fixed them a toasted sandwich and side salad.

'You really don't need to do that. Honestly.'

She looked up. 'Ah, to be honest it will keep me mind off thinking about Eddie, you know? Besides, I like washing up.'

Jed was about to argue that no one in their right in their right mind could actually enjoy washing up, when his mobile rang. It was Imogen.

'Right. I think I can help, but I will need details of all Eddie's race, weights, wins, odds and footage of his races in the last six months.'

Jed moved away into the hallway, out of Bernadette's hearing. 'It's nice to hear from you too, Imogen. I am glad you have decided to help though. Shall I call round tomorrow with the stuff and we can talk more then?'

There was a pause. 'Oh, right. You have someone there. No that's fine.' Jed noticed that Imogen picked up on his cues and understood that he couldn't very well discuss his concerns about Eddie and his honesty or rather lack of it in front of his own mother.

'Yes. I have Eddie's mum staying for bit.'

'Oh, right. That's kind of you.'

'But if you want to meet up tomorrow, eight o'clock?'

Imogen told him her address and he rang off. He resisted the urge to punch the air and wondered what she had made of Eddie's blood test results. Then the phone rang again almost immediately.

'Jed, where have you been? Why haven't you returned my calls?'

It was Arabella, his one time girlfriend. He moved further into the hallway.

'Oh hi. I've just been so busy with everything, that's all. I am a full time jockey now you know. I'm struggling to fit in any sort of social life.'

'Too busy to come to a party with me at the weekend?'

'I'm riding out tomorrow and I've got an early start on Sunday, so I can't this weekend. Besides, Eddie, you remember Eddie O'Neill, well, he's in a coma and I've got his mother staying so there's a lot to sort out.' He could hear the disappointment in her voice. Hell, he hadn't expected their recent encounter to become a regular thing, it was just sex for both of them, wasn't it? Besides, he was really busy and had to spend some time going through Eddie's stuff. He needed to give the whole situation some thought. 'Look. I'll give you a ring when I'm not busy and fix something up in a week or so. That do you?'

'OK. Hope Eddie recovers soon. I read about the accident. It's a shame. He's a nice guy.'

Jed rang off, hoping that Bernadette hadn't overhear him using Eddie's accident as an excuse not to go out. God, what was happening to him? Who would have thought Jed Cavendish would turn out a night on the tiles and a sure thing for an evening investigating his friend's accident with an academic he barely knew? Perhaps, he was beginning to tire of casual relationships?

Despite Jed asking Bernadette to come and go as she please and treat the place as her own and NOT tidy up, he noticed the whole place was spotless when he woke up. The surfaces and floor gleamed and every plate, knife and fork had been washed and tidied away. The whole place smelt of polish and cleaning fluid. She had left him a note to say she had gone to the hospital and made a Bolognese sauce for his tea. Bless, what a lovely woman she was. He busied himself trying to gather the information Imogen had requested and spent some time using the internet to find Eddie's past results detailing the rides, trainers, betting and positions. Bernadette had left him Eddie's key for his cottage and needing a break, he decided to take a drive out there before calling in at Lydia Fox's to ride.

The sun flickered in and out of the trees as he made his way to Eddie's house. The city soon gave way to vast fields and rolling hills. He loved York with its hustle and bustle, vast historic buildings and narrow, cobbled streets, but he had to admit the scenery out here in rural Walton was breath taking. The landscape comprised of large fields edged with trees whose Autumn leaves were such vivid yellows and oranges, it was like a tapestry of rich, vivid spices. He was buzzing a little in anticipation about what he might find at Eddie's cottage. He wondered if the police had been there and decided that they probably hadn't as Bernadette would have mentioned it. Besides, they still seemed fixed on the idea that Eddie's accident was just that, an accident. His mind turned over what he knew so far. Eddie had received a strange call which he had taken, *twelve in the sixth*. He had forgotten to pass the information on, and Eddie had gone on to win on number twelve in the sixth race. And Eddie ended up having a car accident that evening after contacting Jed, incoherent and scared. Then there was the argument between Eddie and Gary. Was that a co-incidence? He thought not. Yet, Eddie was such a straightforward, down the line sort of guy it didn't sit well. He knew in his heart that something was very wrong. God, what was he going to find at Eddie's house and more importantly what should he be looking for?

Eddie lived in the end house in a small row of cottages on the edge of Walton. It was within walking distance of Kieron McLoughlin's yard where he was stable jockey. The cottage looked well kept and unremarkable, apart from a large growth of Virginia creeper that covered the front of the house. Jed fished out the keys from his pocket and unlocked the door. The smell of dust mingled with the scent of sour milk hit him as he walked in. He stepped over a pile of mail, through a narrow hall into the kitchen. There were some coffee cups in the sink and a few plates, plus a half-eaten bowl of cornflakes awash with milk, the source of the foul smell, he decided. He wandered into the sitting room which was neat and tidy with two grey sofas, a large plasma TV and a bookcase full of racing novels, biographies and Timeform books. There was a cabinet to one side with three large drawers whose contents he thought he would look at later. To the rear there was a small conservatory leading to a mainly paved garden.

Upstairs there was a small wet room and two bedrooms. The larger one had built in wardrobes; a double bed, with several photos of horses Eddie had ridden adorning the walls. He suddenly felt terribly sad and voyeuristic wandering around Eddie's house without his knowledge or consent, but what was the alternative? Eddie had trusted him enough to ring him when he was in trouble, so he had to look for clues as to what was going on. He pulled on some gloves, having decided this was the proper thing to do to avoid leaving fingerprints. If the police did visit the property at some point in the future, he didn't want to make their job any harder or become a prime suspect by leaving his prints all over the place. He opened the top drawer of Eddie's bedside cabinet and found a pack of condoms with several missing, cough sweets, a box of aspirins and a mouth wash. Underneath he found several bank statements and some photos. One was of an attractive brunette who smiled into the camera. It looked like it had been taken at a holiday resort, judging by the sunburn on her face and the holiday clothes. A girlfriend he decided, thinking she looked vaguely familiar. He grabbed the bank statements to read later and flicked through Eddie's wardrobe. There were several expensive looking suits hung up, decent shoes and ties, and on the other side casual clothes, riding breeches, boots, undershirts, his hat, body protector and several warm jackets. In another set of drawers was underwear, boxers and socks, a drawer full of aftershave; Gucci and Marc Jacobs for men and several watches. He studied them. There were some expensive brands Omega and Rolex amongst them plus some boxes containing gold cufflinks and some silver ones designed in the shape of a horse. Eddie clearly liked nice things and there was evidence he had spent some money on his appearance, but was it any more than any young man his age? Probably not. Some of the items were probably gifts from friends, family and delighted owners. Eddie was an up and coming jockey, so was getting more and more attention as his career progressed. He was an excellent horseman and managed to get the last ounce out of every horse he rode. It would be entirely likely that he had either won some of these expensive items or been given them by grateful owners.

Downstairs there was more mail in a kitchen drawer and a range of barely used kitchen utensils. It was clear that Eddie was not a cook then. He opened the American style fridge which was full of bottled water, salad, a couple of bottles of champagne, mouldy cheese and natural yoghurt. In the sitting room he found lots of old form books, several Dick Francis novels and a PS4 complete with several games including the latest from FIFA. Eddie was more of a hurling or Irish football fan as he remembered, so he was surprised at this. Just as he was about to leave, he noticed a small framed photograph of the presenter Felicity Hill. She pouted at the camera and looked like she was wearing casual clothes which suggested she was not at work. Jed frowned, wondering if it was a publicity photo. It seemed too casual for that. Perhaps, Eddie's relationship with Felicity had progressed from a flirtation to a full blown relationship? He thought about the condom packet upstairs and wondered. He glanced at his watch and realised he was late for Lydia's. He had a quick look in the cabinet and removed some of the letters, quickly scanning through some of the opened letters. He left with Eddie's bank statements and a handful of his recent unopened post, feeling that he had learned little really. He felt oddly deflated. He had no idea what he'd expected to find, thousands of pounds of used banknotes hidden away somewhere perhaps? He placed the letters in a plastic bag he found in a kitchen drawer, vowing to look at them later. He would also talk to Bernadette about Eddie's girlfriends and find out what the state of play was there.

He had a feeling that nothing much would get past Mrs O'Neill and suspected that though her son lived in another country, she would have some intuitive knowledge about his relationships with the opposite sex.

Chapter 10

Imogen waited for Jed to arrive. Since he had turned up at her office and told her of his suspicions, she hadn't been able to think about much else. In fact, his entire presence unsettled her. It was hard to know why, perhaps a combination of his charm and the fact that he barely knew her and yet was asking for her help. He had made her feel responsible, damn him. The story he had told her she found frightening and oddly compelling. She had heard about Eddie O'Neill's car crash, as it had been widely reported in the press, but there were no other details and the assumption had been that it was simply an accident. But Jed's story of the phone call and the strange message that he forgot to pass onto Eddie, which appeared to amount to an instruction to stop a horse, was alarming. That someone was prepared to injure Eddie because he didn't comply with what was they asked was absolutely terrifying. She was flattered that Jed had sought her help and relieved that he hadn't been lying when he left her that evening. Jed had recognised that her analytical brain would be well suited to solving such a case and she was desperate not to let him or Eddie down. Then, there were the test results. Professional curiosity had got the better of her and she had examined them closely. Imogen had no idea how Jed had acquired them, but they told their own story. It was clear that at the time of the accident, Eddie was NOT dehydrated, and this certainly gave weight to Jed's suspicions. In the back of her mind was also what Marcus had said about the last race at Uttoxeter, which although a throw away comment, fitted perfectly with Jed's theory. If there was a betting scam, how the hell did Marcus hear about it? Was it a coincidence? She wasn't sure and deep down she had real misgivings about what her brother was getting involved in and if she could prevent Marcus from getting in deeper, then so much the better. So, like it or not, she had to help Jed to save Marcus.

She had tidied up her already neat house and sprayed some vanilla air freshener about then busied herself flicking through the TV channels. She discovered that the entire month's racing was available to view retrospectively on certain channels, and there were even more races available to watch, on a website called 'At the Races.' That could be useful. She had placed a bottle of white wine in the fridge and assembled some snacks, crisps and nuts together to help them think. She had also fished out a large pad and a pack of marker pens she used for teaching, to help them make some notes.

Jed arrived at eight on the dot carrying a bag full of Racing Posts, Timeform books and a collection of Eddie's mail. He grinned and kissed both her cheeks in the Continental fashion. The gesture was very naturally performed on his part, yet she felt her cheeks burn in confusion.

'I popped into Eddie's this afternoon and had a look round.' He lifted one plastic bag. 'I came across some bank statements, so I brought them along.' He also took out some lightweight, plastic gloves and handed them to her. 'Best not to leave fingerprints, just in case.'

Imogen nodded. 'Great. I'll have a look through. It's kind of you to put Eddie's mother up. She must be dreadfully worried. Is there any change in his condition?'

Jed shook his head and looked preoccupied. Imogen poured them some wine, tipped out the letters onto the floor and began to sort through them.

'So, I looked at those test results you gave me...'

Jed studied her. 'And...'

Imogen had copied the report and highlighted some of the figures. She pointed to the *serum osmolality* and *blood urea nitrogen* figures. 'They are definitely within normal limits for a man of Eddie's age and weight, I presume he is mid twenties and weighs about ten and a half stone?'

Jed nodded. 'So, he wasn't dehydrated?'

'Not at the time the blood was taken, presumably just after the accident. He probably was earlier on in the day for the race and afterwards drank loads of water, so by the evening his hydration levels were pretty normal.'

Jed nodded thoughtfully. 'So, the accident couldn't have been caused by Eddie having a blackout or feeling dizzy or any of those things due to dehydration?'

'Well, I'd say it was highly unlikely.'

Jed sighed. 'I knew it. It just didn't make any sense. Why haven't the police realised this?'

Imogen shrugged. 'Perhaps they haven't asked the right questions or have just made assumptions….'

Jed nodded. 'OK. Where do we start with all of this?' He gestured at the spread of letters, statements and book. Imogen picked up the bank statements.

'I'll look through these, shall I?''

Jed settled down on the sofa. 'I'll make a start on analysing some of Eddie's races.' His face was grim. Imogen had the distinct feeling that he didn't want to study them for fear of what he might find.

Jed went back over the last year's racing and considered all of Eddie's races in that time whilst Imogen sorted through the letters. She wondered what on earth Jed was looking for and asked how he was going to narrow down his search.

'Which races are you going to look at? Where are you going to start?'

Jed sighed. He seemed to have given the matter a great deal of thought.

'Well, the most obvious way to make money is to back a horse with long odds, and assuming the bookies are good at their job, which they are, we should look at the races where Eddie was riding the favourite. If it didn't win and a horse with long odds did then, those races would be worth studying in more depth. It could mean that Eddie pulled those races.'

Imogen considered this. 'Right. How many favourites did he ride that lost?'

'I have looked at last season and this season and there is around ten altogether.'

Imogen nodded. The world of racing was completely alien to her.

'Would that number be reasonable, would you say?'

Jed shrugged. 'Could be.' He smiled, and she had felt momentarily disarmed. 'It's not like statistics you know. Horses are not entirely predictable and can have an off day, not be in the mood, feel under the weather, have soreness, pain, anything really.'

Imogen realised that she did feel much more at home with figures which did exactly what they were supposed to do.

'OK. I'll look through the statements for any obvious themes.'

Jed pulled out a prepared list of Eddie's races. He had ridden about a hundred winners over this season, but he was interested in the ten races where the favourites he had ridden lost. Some of these races were available on TV catch up and all were available online. Of the ten favourites Eddie had ridden, Jed chose four races to review, where a rank outsider came through to win.

'So, how would a jockey pull a race and not make it obvious? I suppose races are scrutinised?' Imogen was genuinely curious.

'Well, you might expect to see a jockey perhaps falling off when he could have maintained his seat, not really riding out at the finish, maybe taking the wrong line to waste time, anything like that.'

'OK. Well, your expert knowledge is definitely needed there.' Not for the first time she thought that all jockeys needed their heads read. It was dangerous enough to ride without deliberately falling off and trying to lose a race. She turned back to the statements.

Eddie was quite meticulous in that his bank statements were in date order, which at least helped. Imogen went through his income and outgoings considering utilities such as gas, electricity, phone bills, council tax, rent, loans and so on. The statements went back about a year or so, although there were one or two missing. There were also some credit cards and loan statements. She went through the expenditure trying to make sense of it and work out what Eddie's outgoings were, to see if there were any unusual patterns. She leafed through several statements and made some notes. At the same time, she was aware of Jed frowning and replaying some of the races again and again.

'Have you found something?'

Jed moved his head from side to side, uncertainly. 'Not really.' He watched the race back and pointed at the screen. 'In this race, Eddie is riding Kittiwake and he loses ground by trying to make some space for himself. Look, he pulls wide to position his horse.'

Jed pointed at the TV screen and pursed his lips. 'Mind you, that is what I'd have done. But the horse is looking jaded and Eddie realises he's not going to win but tries to push on for a place anyway.'

Imogen watched as all the jockeys, Eddie amongst them, rode towards the finish, whips raised, rocking backward and forward as they urged their horses on. Eddie's efforts looked just as vigorous as the other jockeys, but his horse faded in the home run.

Imogen shrugged. 'It looks fine to me, but then again what do I know?'

Jed analysed another race where the horse, Marmalade, slightly pecked on landing and Eddie fell to the ground over the horse's shoulder.

'Well, that was just unlucky. There was no way he could have stayed aboard there. But again, he's on the favourite and the damned outsider, that grey there, comes up to win.'

Imogen thought the fall looked pretty grim, but Eddie rolled up into a ball and just managed to avoid being trampled by several tons of horseflesh. Again, she found herself marvelling at the risks they were prepared to take.

'How often do jockeys fall, on average?'

Jed shrugged. 'I think someone calculated it to be once every fourteen or so rides. The majority are straightforward, but those involving a horse fall are the most dangerous, because the jockey could be crushed.' He noticed her expression and grinned. 'It goes with the territory.'

Imogen shook her head and continued poring over Eddie's accounts.

'Look. That's Dominion at Doncaster. Again, Eddie is riding the favourite, but he starts well and runs out of puff at the end.' Jed pointed to the finish. 'There's nothing wrong with Eddie's finish, he's trying, but Dominion looks to have had a knock and hit a fence further back. Probably has a minor leg injury. Bet he was lame the next day, the horse looks slightly uncomfortable there. Look.'

Jed pointed at the horse as he finished the race well down the field. Imogen squinted at the screen. The horse looked to be moving like any other in the race. There was obviously so much more to this racing malarkey, she decided. Mind you, Jed would no doubt struggle in her job, analysing data at the University.

Jed looked at another race and then switched off the TV, his long legs stretched out in front of him. He actually looked relieved.

'Well, if Eddie has pulled any of these horses, he's done an excellent job of it, because I can't see any evidence. They're the ones where the rank outsider won, but I will look at the other six. How about you? Did you find anything?'

Imogen flicked through the bank statements.

'Well, I will need to study the accounts in more detail. Does Eddie's cottage come with the job, do you know?'

'Not as far as I know. He was apprenticed to Kieran and took over as stable jockey. He used to live in the lads' hostel, but probably moved out when he was made stable jockey.'

'Did he had to do that, or was he given the choice?'

Jed shrugged. 'He probably wanted more privacy or something, he would be on a retainer and earning more. It's a natural progression. As you can imagine, the hostels are for stable staff, usually.'

'OK. I'll need to look through them in more detail, I'm afraid.'

Jed paused. 'Well, I'm as sure as I can be that Eddie rode those races honestly, but I will look at the others. I'd have thought though, that the ones where a horse with really long odds wins, would be the starting point. '

'Wouldn't that arouse too much suspicion?'

'Maybe.' Jed nodded to his notebook where he had written down the names of the horses whose races he had just looked at. Kittiwake, Marmalade, Dominion and Super Trooper. They were all trained by Kieron McLoughlin. This wasn't surprising as Eddie was his stable jockey. He began to search for the other six favourites Eddie had ridden. He made a list of the trainers of the horses that had won when he had lost, to see if there were any patterns.

'Do you think the trainers of the winning horse would be in on the scam?'

Jed looked uncertain. 'I'm not sure but look, the list of the trainers who won when the favourites didn't, is pretty diverse. I can't see any obvious patterns.'

Imogen followed his gaze. 'Except there are three for someone called Hugh Mitchell. Look.'

'Oh yes. He trains up by Lydia Fox, a female trainer.'

'What do you know about Hugh Mitchell?'

'I don't know much about him, but I'll ask Lydia when I next see her.' His eyes widened as he thought of something. 'In fact, even better I have been asked to ride one of his horses next week, my agent rang me about it.'

There seemed to be no other real themes and Jed had yet to examine the other races. Imogen pointed to the other list he had made.

'What's this list?'

'That's a list of the stewards who were on duty.'

Imogen pointed at one name that cropped up for each race meeting where the favourites had lost. 'So, who is Richard Kendrick?'

'A stipendiary steward who covers a few racecourses.'

'Do you know him?'

Jed nodded. 'By reputation, I've not been before him. From what I hear, he's switched on, firm but fair.'

'What does a stipendiary steward do actually?' It occurred to Imogen that the world of racing was full of strange terminology.

'They advise the other stewards and order blood tests on horses, decide on stewards' inquiries, look at riding breaches and generally uphold the integrity of racing. They cover racecourses in a geographical area and are employed by the BHA to assist the other stewards who are volunteers. I made a list of the stewards officiating on the day, but as there was no stewards' inquiries, then it's probably irrelevant.'

Imogen frowned. That was a blind alley then. They were definitely missing something. 'Did Eddie have any enemies, anyone who might want to harm him?'

The thought appalled Jed. 'God, no. He is very popular. Everyone loves Eddie, he's a charmer, funny, likeable. Everyone's favourite Irishman.'

Imogen privately thought that Jed had a very rosy view of Eddie. People were rarely as they appeared. Charming, funny, likeable. The same could be said of her brother Marcus, yet in reality he had a much darker side with many enemies, one of whom had even harmed her. Her fingers reached for her scar.

'Are you sure about that? How about someone who Eddie took over from, disgruntled punters, another jockey, someone who maybe thinks Eddie took his rides?'

84

Jed looked askance. 'Gary McKay? Eddie did take over as stable jockey at McLoughlins. But God, no. Gary's a bit of a misery guts, but that's it. He wouldn't have it in him to seriously harm anyone. Besides, Eddie's car accident must be related to his winning the sixth race on number twelve when he was supposed to lose it. *Twelve in the sixth.'*

Imogen nodded bleakly. 'We are missing something, we must be. Maybe, we just need to look harder at the facts and look at the patterns? It will become clear, I'm sure.'

Jed looked thoughtful. 'Well, how about you continue looking at the bank stuff and I'll study those other races and maybe drive to the health club where Eddie arranged to meet me. Perhaps, someone was with him or saw something, maybe there's a clue that the police missed?'

'Do we even know how the accident actually happened? Was there another car involved?'

'I don't think so, but that is a very good question. I'll make some inquiries.'

Imogen peered at one of the pieces of papers, her mind in overdrive as her mind processed the information.

'You know when you last rode in the race that Eddie won, after you took that 'twelve in the sixth' call, where did you finish exactly?'

'Oh, you mean at the Uttoxeter meeting? He beat me narrowly by about three lengths or so, and the second placed horse was a length ahead of me.'

Imogen's gaze was sharp. 'So, you were third?' Jed nodded. 'OK. Has it occurred to you that whoever was second was meant to win?'

'Oh, you mean Gary McKay?'

'Yes. Who was he riding for, who trained his horse?'

'Oh, I see what you mean.' Jed had paled. 'It was another horse trained by Hugh Mitchell.'

Imogen looked at him meaningfully. 'So, do you think Gary McKay knew he was supposed to win? Is he involved or even THE Mr Big in the operation?'

Jed could only stare at her in horror.

'Gary was annoyed with Eddie at the end of the race, so maybe…'

Was Gary McKay behind the scam? He had a grudge against Eddie, so he had a motive of sorts. Then he felt rather lightheaded. He remembered what Bernadette had said.

'Listen Imogen, a Scottish man went to visit Eddie, Bernadette told me. Supposing that was Gary?' The blood drained from his face. 'Supposing he didn't go to wish Eddie well, suppose he wanted to find out when he was likely to wake come out of his coma…'

Imogen gasped. 'God, so he could stop him talking?'

The answer hung in the air between them, unspoken, like an unexploded bomb.

Suddenly they both realised the enormity of the task ahead, the threat to Eddie and also the risks they were placing themselves in.

Jed sighed. 'We'd better get on with it then…'

Chapter 11

On Sunday morning Jed was summoned to Cavendish Hall to see his parents. His mother, Caroline, had phoned and in a plaintive tone, asked him to call in.

'It's just we've hardly seen you since you've been riding, darling.' It was on the tip of Jed's tongue to bite back and suggest that if they came to the races, then they might see rather more of him, but he decided against it.

As he drove up to the elegant Cavendish Hall, which was a three-storey brick-built Queen Anne mansion, he reflected on the fact that he was lucky indeed to be only the younger son of a Lord and merely an Honourable, a title he never intended to use. He considered that the upkeep of the property was a millstone around his brother Hugh's neck, but being the elder son and the one set to inherit the title and land, he had worked tirelessly to uphold the family tradition and the maintenance of the historic house. Poor Hugh, he hadn't had the choice of career and yet he had been an excellent polo player and now only had time for the odd chukka. His sister being the eldest and a mere female, was expected to marry a rich, suitable man, according to her parents, but Milly had decided to, 'stuff the lot of them' and pursue an academic career in Psychology. Her feminist ideology meant that she was rather opposed to marriage. Still, her partner Jack was a great chap, but he probably wasn't what his parents would consider 'suitable'. Whereas, Hugh had married Sophie, who was a good sort, even if she did dress like someone twice her age. Sophie favoured tweed skirts, twin sets and pearls. His parents adored her and regarded her as 'very appropriate'. Jed sincerely hoped that Hugh and Sophie would soon knock out a brood of children and take the pressure off him and Milly, but there was no sign of this so far.

Lord and Lady Cavendish were waiting for him in the drawing room. His mother was sipping sherry whilst his father drank whiskey and flicked absently through a car magazine. They were both smartly dressed.

'Darling, how lovely to see you.' His mother rose as he kissed her cheek and his father shook his hand stiffly.

'Splendid, old chap. Fancy a drink?'

'No, I'm driving.' His father sniffed rather dismissively. Like so many of his generation, he frequently drank and saw this as no impediment to driving.

'You are staying for lunch, aren't you darling, only Mrs B is cooking beef wellington, your favourite. I particularly asked her, you know.'

Jed patted his stomach. 'No, I'm riding at Taunton tomorrow, so I can't.'

Lady Cavendish made a face and patted the sofa next to her. 'Well, do come and tell us how it's all going. I've got quite addicted to that Racing Programme. I am not a fan of that new presenter, though, what's her name?'

His father had brightened considerably. 'Felicity Hill, I think she's a breath of fresh air, myself.'

His mother was clearly not convinced and rolled her eyes. 'Well, you seem to be doing well, darling. Awful about that friend of yours, Eddie wasn't it?'

'Yes, he's in a coma.'

Lady Cavendish looked anguished. 'Oh dear. How dreadful. I do worry about you. You will be careful, won't you?'

Jed reassured them that yes, he would, but that Eddie had been injured in a car accident which had nothing to do with riding.

'Now, how is dear Arabella, only I had Leticia on the phone and she tells me you haven't seen much of her since you've been riding.'

So that was it. Arabella Winter was the daughter of his mother's good friend Leticia Winter and clearly, Arabella had been complaining that Jed hadn't been playing ball.

'Well, it's true. Now I'm a professional, I have to ride out for trainers, travel a great deal and then I've been busy with Eddie.'

His mother was seriously displeased. 'Busy, how? The man is in a coma, for goodness sake, you've just told us…'

'Well, I have been visiting.'

His mother's face softened. 'Oh. You were always a sensitive boy. It's just that if you're not serious about the gel then the least you can do is stay away from her, darling. It's only fair. '

'Only fair,' echoed his father. It was one of the rare moments when his parents were in agreement. Usually, low level bickering was their default setting.

Well, perhaps, I will then, Jed thought, deciding not to voice his opinions aloud. Arabella must have been far more upset than he realised about his failure to stay in touch. He couldn't quite square this with her party girl image, somehow. Perhaps, she was beginning to tire of that life or more likely she wanted what she couldn't have. He had no doubt that she would lose interest if he suddenly began chasing her. He attempted to change the subject.

'Where's Hugh and Sophie?'

'With the in-laws, I think. The wedding business is going splendidly, though. Loads of happy couples and plenty of room for another Cavendish,' replied his father pointedly.

'When you've had your fun,' added his mother. 'Though, Milly shows no sign of giving up teaching.'

Jed decided to put her right. 'Lecturing, you mean. I hope she doesn't give it up, she's studying for a PhD, you know. She's doing very well.'

Two pairs of eyes surveyed him with disappointed expressions, and he wondered how long he could cope with this two-pronged attack. He steered the conversation to more neutral topics before heading off.

'Any tips for tomorrow? 'asked his father hopefully as he was leaving.

'Lydia Fox is an up and coming trainer, so anything from her yard might be worth a bet.' He couldn't resist trying to promote Lydia's cause.

'Lydia Fox, eh? Right you are.'

'Yes, that's right. I rather rate her actually.' His father seemed to take this in. Although, his parents were not racehorse owners themselves, plenty of their friends were and it would not do any harm to try and fill some of Lydia's empty stables.

Taunton was a popular racecourse set in the Somerset countryside, well known for its incline towards the finish, which had caught out many a jockey deciding to make their run for home too early. Jed had been up early to make the long journey but hoped it would be worth it. He had four runners, two for Lydia Fox, one for

Kieran McLoughlin and another for Hugh Mitchell. He had looked over Lydia's two yesterday and had a pretty good idea what they were like. As he had chatted, he had almost confided in Lydia about Eddie's situation, but couldn't quite bring himself to discuss it openly. He had no idea what others thought of Eddie and didn't want to jeopardise his comeback, if he made a full recovery that was. Jed was still feeling angry and annoyed about the whole thing. He and Imogen had found few real clues, and he was feeling frustrated and annoyed with the lack of progress. He had gone back to his house in York, swearing and cursing in the car, knowing full well he couldn't say anything to Bernadette either. He had promised to 'suss out' Hugh Mitchell, go back to the health club and then meet up again. He hadn't yet had time to go through the other six races but intended to soon. Imogen was going to go through the statements to make sure she hadn't missed anything, but there didn't seem to be anything obvious. Jed was glad that he had a busy afternoon coming up, anything to distract him from Eddie and his predicament.

As usual the weighing room was full of banter interspersed with some juicy gossip. Jake Horton, a jockey with a reputation for hard work and fearless riding was especially upbeat.

'It seems,' said Tristan Davies as he watched Jake, 'that Felicity Hill has switched her attention to him now that Eddie is ill. Poor sod.' Jed didn't know if he was referring to Jake or Eddie.

'Was it serious, this thing between Eddie and Felicity?' He watched as Jake began loudly telling them about a party he had been at with Felicity and about all the celebrities who had been there. Probably, the sort of circles Arabella mixed within. In fact, this was probably the party she'd invited him to, Jed realised.

Tristan shrugged. 'I doubt it. She seems to flirt with a lot of the guys.'

Jed wondered what Eddie's take on things might be. He thought back to the photo Eddie had of her at his cottage. Perhaps, Felicity handed out publicity photos to lots of people? She certainly seemed like someone who would be into self promotion, or how else had she managed to land such a plum job?

'Hey. I'm riding for Hugh Mitchell today. I've not ridden for him before, what's he like?'

'I've never actually met him. His assistant is usually at the races, I think. His name is Anton, think he's French or something like that... Has different ideas, if you know what I mean. I suppose they do things differently in France. They've had some good winners though.'

Jed did know. While he thought about it, he decided to ask about the steward, Richard Kendrick.

'What's Richard Kendrick like as a steward, have you had any dealings with him?'

Tristan nodded. 'One or two. He's fairly recently appointed, rich wife so they say. I was up before them for obstructing a horse and overuse of the whip.' He shrugged. 'But he seems OK, a bit of a stickler. I'm sure you'll come across him sooner or later.'

Jed grinned. The stewards did police racing and firmly upheld the conduct of jockeys. For example, you could only hit a horse eight times in a hurdle race and only five times within the last furlong. If a jockey was in with a shout at the end, then they had to be careful not to get carried away.

Lydia Fox's horses both ran well; Picardy finished just out of the placings in sixth and Just A Minute showed considerable improvement from his last race, finishing fourth. Kieran McLoughlin, who usually had Eddie ride for him, was keen to discuss Eddie's situation.

'Is there any progress?' Jed shook his head, watching Kieran's face fall. 'Poor lad. In a bloody car accident too! We've been to see him of course. Geraldine is really cut up about it.'

Geraldine, Kieran's wife, stood with her husband, her face pale and anxious. She also looked vaguely familiar, but Jed couldn't recall where he had seen her. He knew it would come to him.

Kieran gave him his instructions in a low voice.

'Anyway, just keep yourself in the running and if he has any more puff, then pick them off one by one.'

Celtic Warrior didn't have any more puff and faded in the final furlong, beaten into third place by a short head. Jed felt he might do better over nearly three miles rather than the usual two mile hurdle and explained this to Kieran.

'He really didn't have anything left and I didn't want to push him for a place.'

Kieran nodded. 'Yes, very sensible. Well, if you're free, I'd like you ride a few others? I am struggling with Eddie being out of action.' Jed felt a little uneasy, but it wasn't as though Eddie was going to be back any time soon. He felt the need to clarify the situation.

'Well, I can't discuss it with Eddie but of course, he's still going to be your stable jockey when he's back.' It was more of a statement than a question.

'That's right. I know you and he are friends, but you'd just be keeping his saddle warm, that's all. '

'Great, then, in that case, I'd be delighted.'

Kieran clapped him on the back. 'Good lad. That's grand.'

Jed didn't get to meet Hugh Mitchell and as Tristan had predicted it was his assistant, Anton Du Pre who was saddling up. He was certainly a man of little words and in terms of giving instructions, he was what might be described as very brief.

'Just run. OK? He's, how you say, jeune, hmm, a little green...'e needs the race.' From this and poring over the Racing Post, Jed had deduced that this was Periwinkle's first time over hurdles having won and been placed over the flat.

Periwinkle was a beautiful dapple grey gelding and as Anton had said, was rather green. He jumped like a stag but became rather frightened when another horse came close to him, causing him to veer to the left over a fence and peck on landing sending Jed over his head. All jockeys are adept at minimising damage to themselves by rolling up into a tight ball and Jed was no exception. Damn. The horse had showed promise otherwise, which was what he tried to explain to Anton.

'I think he has scope. Would you like me to come and school him?' Jed suggested.

Anton blinked and frowned uncomprehendingly.

Jed tried again. 'Perhaps, I can ride him at home, chez toi...' Anton nodded and clapped him on the back.

'Oui. You ride, chez moi? C'est superbe.'

'What day?'

Anton shrugged. 'A tout moment... How you say, anytime.'

Jed smiled back, thinking he definitely needed to brush up on his schoolboy French. He hadn't really got the time, but at least he would get to have a look at Mitchell's set up and find out a bit more about him. He might even get to meet the elusive Hugh Mitchell himself. At least now he had an 'in'.

On his way back home, he called in at 'Hot Bodies', the gym where he previously waited to meet Eddie. He was greeted by a wall of heat as he entered the glass doors and waited whilst the young receptionist checked some cards and answered some queries from a queue of customers. He was unsure how to play it, just ask for copies of the CCTV of the car park on that evening and see if there was anything suspicious on them. But, how on earth was he going to get the staff to hand it over without proper police ID? Surely, the police had already checked the footage, if they had anything about them?

Eventually, after the queue subsided and he was face to face with a pretty blonde girl, wearing a bored expression that brightened as soon as Jed came into view. He flashed her a bright smile.

'Hello there. I really need a big favour. My friend Eddie O'Neill is a member here and was involved in a car accident when he left. I just need to find out what he did that evening, who he met and so on…' The girl looked instantly wary, so he added.' I am working with the police, but on behalf of the British Horseracing Authority. Eddie is a jockey, you see, so I need to make sure he wasn't involved in anything that could contravene racing rules.' He fished in his pocket for his professional jockey ID and flashed it at her and hoped for the best. 'Purely routine, of course.' Her blue eyes inspected him, taking in his smart suit and jacket he had changed into since riding.

'Well, anything like that would have to go through the manager, Mr Marshall.'

Damn. He sincerely hoped she wasn't going to make things difficult. At this point, the doors swung open, blasting him with cold air, as a group of lads entered. They waited in line behind Jed. The receptionist eyed the queue and started to look a little flustered.

'Look. I'm not asking for sensitive information, just to find out what Eddie did on Saturday and who he hangs around with, that's all.'

The queue built up again as more young men came in.

'What was his name again?'

'Eddie O'Neill.'

The receptionist typed in his name into her computer, as her blue tipped ridiculously long nails ran over the keys.

'Well, he has a full membership, which offers him access to the gym, sauna and pool. He has had some individual sessions with Wayne, our top instructor. He's a regular, that's all I can tell you.'

Well, it was a start, thought Jed.

He beamed at the girl whose badge told him her name was Sacha.

'Thanks, Sacha. Is Wayne in?'

The fingers darted over the keyboard. 'No, he works Mondays, Wednesdays and Fridays, nine to five. He's at our other gym across town on Tuesday and Thursdays. '

'Does Wayne have a surname?'

'Jones.'

'Thank you. You've been very helpful. Can I grab a coffee?'

Sacha's eyes slid to the queue that was about six deep, noisy and on the verge of becoming restless. Sacha paused and came to a decision.

'The café is closed now, but the drinks machine is through there.'

'Great. Thanks.' Jed winked at Sacha who flushed.

Once inside, Jed fed the machine the various change required and sat down in the café, watching various people come and go. On the table to one side was a group of rather loud, muscle bound young men who, judging from their conversation, were about to undo all their good work by heading off to the pub.

Jed studied them as he sipped his drink then and approached them.

'Hi there. Sorry to intrude. Do any of you know a chap called Eddie O' Neill? He's an Irish jockey who comes here regularly…'

A dark haired, young man with a crew cut gave Jed a speculative look. 'Oh, the Irish lad, good guy, always trying to lose weight?'

'That's the one. Only I'm a friend of his, a fellow jockey. Did any of you see him last Saturday, only he was involved in a car accident and I just wondered if any of you had seen anything or had noticed anything unusual about him?'

Several of the group shook their heads. 'Nah. He seemed fine.'

An auburn haired lad with a spotty complexion nodded, stifling a smile. He elbowed his friend. Clearly a joker, Jed decided.

'Well, Ian here was just mentioning the strange lights on the Market Leighton road on Saturday. Why don't you tell this man all about it? Perhaps it was a UFO or something, Ian.'

Ian was blond, slight and clearly had been ribbed about this before. The taller lad could not resist opening him up to ridicule again, in front of a total stranger.

'Shut up, Mike. I did see some strange lights as I was coming into York that evening. I was almost blinded by them, then the lights vanished, just like that.'

'Sure it wasn't a tractor muck spreading in the dark or something?' asked Jed.

Ian shook his head. 'No, it was too bright, blinding almost and then it just disappeared.'

One of the other lads started humming the 'X files' music and Ian glared at him, a flush spreading over his face.

Jed smiled, feeling a bit sorry for Ian. He decided to humour him.

'What time was this?'

Ian frowned. 'Well, I was coming into York for a night out, so it would have been about half eight. I came in on the back road.'

Jed nodded thinking that was the route Eddie had taken. Still the lights could have been anything.

'Was there anything else, did Eddie seem OK to you, not worried or anxious about anything?'

'Nah. Just the usual about trying to keep his weight down, that was all.' Mike studied him. 'He's a good bloke Eddie, give him our best, won't you? Was he badly injured?'

Jed studied them. They obviously hadn't seen the news.

'Yes. He's unfortunately in a coma.' Shock registered on the sea of faces as Jed thanked them and left. It was clear that none of them really knew Eddie or had noticed anything significant. The lights Ian spoke about had to be from a tractor, a farmer working in the dark. Clearly an industrious type working late. He shook his head at Ian's naivety. Probably, he had watched too many Sci Fi movies. Damn. He was still no further on.

Chapter 12

Imogen spent some time studying the statements and going through the other letters. There were no signs of extravagant expenditure which puzzled her. In fact, there was very little sign of money being spent at all. She went through each of the statements noticing that in the early ones there were several direct debits set up for council tax, gas, electricity, telephone and water rates, but in the later statements, the direct debits were cancelled and there were no corresponding payments that covered them. Some people, she knew, disliked direct debits because if you accrued credit, then it was very hard to get back your own money from the companies who earned interest on it. Yet, there were no regular payments that had replaced them. Eddie had to pay his bills like everyone else, surely? She looked for patterns in expenditure, but this didn't make any sense. The direct debits stopped about five months ago. Perhaps, he had a girlfriend or someone else who moved in with him who took over the bills or more likely he used another account in order to pay his bills. But there was very little in the way of outgoings anyway, none for food, sundries, even fuel and she knew jockeys travelled a great deal from racecourse to racecourse. Eddie was no exception. As she was flicking through the envelopes a piece of paper fluttered to the floor. She bent to pick it up and found it was a photo. When she studied it was a grainy image of two people embracing. The photo showed the back of the man's head and shoulders and the woman's face, framed with a halo of dark hair was clearly visible. The photo looked like it had been taken from a long distance using a telephoto lens. The photos showed both their bare shoulders which suggested they were naked or partially clothed. Imogen's heart leapt as she realised that she could be looking at the image that was being used to blackmail Eddie, if indeed it was Eddie in the photo. She wondered who the woman was and guessed she must be engaged or married to someone else. There must be some reason why someone had gone to those lengths to photograph the couple. She pulled out her mobile and texted Jed as she pondered on what she had found. The couple were photographed through an old fashioned sash window, which was covered with a red leaved creeping plant which grew around the window frame. It occurred to Imogen that unless the man was identifiable in some way, that it would be totally useless as an instrument of blackmail. So, she scrutinised the man's image for any signs of his identity. It was then that she noticed that one of his hands, his left, was resting on the girl's shoulder and a he wore a signet ring on his little finger. Perhaps, it wasn't Eddie? She was sure Jed would know if Eddie regularly wore such a ring.

Another possibility came to her regarding the lack of outgoings shown in the statements. It was so obvious she wondered why she hadn't seen it before, especially since she noticed that substantial amounts of Eddie's wages had been transferred into a savings account over the last few months. Almost all of it, in fact. The timing of these deposits and the cancellation of the direct debits coincided exactly. It was as clear as the nose on her face when she thought it through. Eddie had another source of income and Imogen guessed that it was the backhanders that he was being paid, presumably in cash, for pulling horses. He was using this to pay bills, rent and other expenses, so he could save all his wages. It also meant that it was the perfect way of laundering money as the notes would be difficult, almost impossible, to trace. Unless there was another bank account which it didn't seem that there was, it looked increasingly likely that Jed's theory about Eddie taking bribes to pull races was correct, and she'd like to bet that the bribes were paid in cash.

Her thoughts turned to her brother and what he had said. She wondered if Marcus might unwittingly have some knowledge of the gang or perhaps prisoners in general were privy to all sorts of information about criminal activities? He had mentioned the last race at Uttoxeter, what was it he had said? *I would have won more if it wasn't for the sixth race at Uttoxeter.* The phrase that Jed had heard when he picked up Eddie's phone came back to her. *Twelve in the sixth.* It had to be the same race meeting that took place on the same day as Eddie's accident. It was too much of a coincidence. She was visiting the prison again on Saturday and had promised to take her mother. If Marcus knew something about the racing scam, might he also know who was behind Eddie's so called accident? She would casually drop Eddie's name into the conversation and see if there was any reaction. As his older sister, she was confident that she could read Marcus's body language. It was a skill honed to perfection over the years.

Imogen struggled to concentrate on work. She was going through some new figures and inputting the data. She still hadn't heard from Jed and disappointment about their lack of progress was gnawing away at her. She was beginning to see bloody horses everywhere. She willed herself to concentrate on the task in hand. She was looking at the long term use of a drug used to help combat cystitis by neutralising the highly acidic urine associated with the infection. The ingredients contained little of interest and were mainly comprised of sodium bicarbonate. Several research articles extolled the virtues of taking this substance, a major component in baking powder, as a medicine. Other benefits included a dose a day to prevent influenza, as a toothpaste, deodorant and a recommendation that baking powder could enhance athletic performance in terms of endurance by neutralising lactic acid which causes cramp, hence allowing the athlete to perform well for longer. Idly she wondered if this would work in horses and when she completed an internet search, she came across some reference to it specifically in racehorses. The practice of giving this to horses was called milkshaking and though it wouldn't necessarily help with a horse's speed, it could certainly improve their stamina by neutralising the effect of lactic acid and delaying its build up. Then, she realised she was becoming obsessed. A cold chill descended as she realised the lengths that people would go to cheat within horseracing. She had wondered if Jed's suspicions about Eddie were far fetched, but this suggested that he was probably right. People were prepared to take extraordinary risks in the pursuit of money, she supposed and in racing it was possible to make a fortune on betting, especially if you were able to influence the results in small and subtle ways without it being detected.

Jed texted her back and they arranged to meet the following week, which suited her because she realised she might have even more to tell him, as she was visiting Marcus. As usual, her mother was solicitous and keen to make apologies for their father. He couldn't even face visiting his son in prison and it was hard to see Marcus's face light up as she and her mother walked into the room, his eyes pulled as though some magnetic force behind them, only to dim once again when he realised his father had not put in an appearance. Imogen noticed a man with an angular face and restless, watchful eyes, an older harmless looking man, a beefy, much tattooed man and the grey haired professional looking man who looked completely out of place amongst the other inmates. This was the man she had seen previously, and he had the same two young men, complete with baseball caps, sitting at his table. She couldn't help wondering about them, who the man was and what he had done to warrant imprisonment. Again, her party were sitting at the next table. As her gaze flickered back to Marcus, she noticed one of the young men passing a mars bar over to the older man who pocketed it quickly. He must just like them and not be able to get them, she decided. That was the second time she had noticed them passing mars bars to him. She supposed for someone in prison, these small comforts could make all the difference.

Her mother was determinedly upbeat and had spent some time researching career opportunities, so she spent some time explaining various options to Marcus.

'And of course, Imogen is still checking the University website so if anything comes up there, then she'll let you know.' Imogen nodded, wishing her mother didn't make it sound like she was devoting her life to finding her brother a job.

'So how are things at the University?' Marcus asked.

'Fine. I went to dinner with my boss and his girlfriend and met some interesting people. Remember me telling you I'd met Jed Cavendish, well, he was telling me about Eddie O'Neill, you know, the jockey who had that horrible car accident. He's in a coma apparently. He may not pull through, actually.'

Marcus frowned and looked around him. He said in a low voice. 'Yeah, heard about that. Shame.'

On the next table, one of the young men had stretched out his thin legs in front of him and was leaning back on his chair, poised, almost as though he was listening. Surely not, she was just imagining things.

'Horses are so dangerous. I'm glad neither of you were interested in riding,' commented her mother.

'He was injured in a car accident, though, mum,' persisted Imogen, her eyes never leaving Marcus's face, 'just after he'd won in the last race at Uttoxeter.'

Marcus leaned forwards, a muscle throbbing his cheek. He glanced at the table besides him and lowered his voice. His Adam's apple was bobbing dangerously, a sure sign he was nervous.

'Yeah well, those jockeys love speeding in cars as much as with horses. He was probably racing other cars on the road, I shouldn't wonder.'

Imogen pondered upon this, wondering whether to say anything more. Marcus was looking at her in a challenging sort of a manner, but he was also twitching and looked rather uncomfortable. He was trying to hide it, of course, but it looked like the tension was seeping out of him in the form of jerky movements, however hard he tried to conceal it.

'Of course, the police are looking into the accident, or so I hear,' she added lightly.

Her mother looked from one to the other. 'Well. The police will do their job then, won't they? Now, is it time for a cup of tea, dear?'

The visit continued, and her mother filled Marcus in on all the local gossip, what the neighbours were up to and how they had all asked after him. Imogen doubted this very much. But she could have sworn that Marcus knew more than he was letting on about Eddie's 'accident'. She was his older sister and she had always known when he was lying. She remembered when he protested his innocence after he had scribbled on her Barbie dolls or even worse in her books and then denied all knowledge. He had a way of setting his head, as though daring her to contradict him and the jerky movements were all part of him trying to feign nonchalance, but he couldn't quite carry it off. She resolved to tell Jed, but she baulked at the realisation that she would also need to tell him about Marcus and why he was in prison. She hated having to explain about him because that would inevitably lead to more questions and then she would need to tell him about the attack on her. Just describing what happened made her feel like a victim all over again and she hated that more than anything.

Chapter 13

Jed went in to ride at Lydia Fox's place again. As he drew into the yard, there were a couple of young girls grooming the horses. They looked up at Jed as he got out of the car. The girls were clearly not professional staff judging by their age, fourteen or so and by the inappropriate tracksuits they were wearing and their false nails, he noticed with wry amusement. Lydia saw him draw up and gave him a warm smile. The girls studied Jed with undisguised interest.

'This is the jockey, Jed Cavendish. Jed, this is Chantelle and Lisa who are helping out today.'

Jed nodded and smiled. The girls giggled and smoothed down their hair. One of them had her dark hair scraped into a bun and the other had blonde hair pulled back into a ponytail. They reminded Jed of Felicity Hill, with their false nails and fake tan. He was curious to know what they were doing there as they looked different to other horsey girls of their age.

'Hey, Lydia, what time is Daz coming to pick us up?' asked the taller of the two girls.

'Oh, a bit later. But don't forget that you are having a lesson this afternoon.' The girls brightened immediately.

'OK, cool.'

They walked out of earshot.

'Your staff look very young and not particularly expert.' Jed nodded to Chantelle, who was attempting and failing, to plait one of the horse's manes, her ridiculously long nails proving to be a huge impediment to the task.

Lydia laughed. 'Oh no, they're not staff as such. They claim to be horse mad so they 'help out' in return for a ride on Ears. He's such a sweetheart, even my gran could ride him. I give them the occasional lesson. Their parents couldn't afford them, and it keeps them out of trouble, I suppose.'

Jed nodded. How like Lydia to be so accommodating and helpful to some local kids. Still, it was probably one of the reasons she was struggling to make it in the racing game, she was just too nice.

They spent the morning schooling a couple of her horses and when they had finished guiding a couple of youngsters over a series of hurdles she had rigged up in her paddock, they had a break. Lydia invited him into her bungalow for a coffee. The place was just like her, tidy and neat. In fact, it had the look of someone who had just moved in and had an echoey quality as it was incredibly spartan inside.

She came through from the kitchen with two brimming mugs and also produced a large chocolate cake.

'Fancy a slice?' She flapped her hands. 'Sorry, I always forget about the tyranny of the scales. And I love baking. Never mind, I'm sure the girls will have some later.'

She helped herself to a slice and took a sip of coffee.

'So, what do you make of my yard?'

'Very organised and tidy.' He wanted to ask about the empty stables and tried to think of a way of doing this. 'I'm sure you'll do well. I always like riding for you, your horses are well schooled and not like some of the kamikaze rides we take from some trainers. It's a shame you haven't got more horses. For someone with your skill, I'm amazed that you haven't got people queuing up to place their horses with you.'

She laughed then her face became serious. 'Yeah, thanks for the vote of confidence. You're a real pal, but as you can see, I've still got a few empty stables. It's not easy being a woman in a man's world, you know.'

Jed was surprised at her vehemence. She was usually so composed.

'Nonsense. It's about making progress every year and this year you've got more horses than last year, and you'll have more winners than last year. You'll get there in the end.'

Lydia brightened. 'Yeah, you're probably right. Don't mind me, I'm just having a crap day.' She ran her fingers through her brown hair and shook her head, as though trying to get rid of some demons. It probably was hard being a woman in racing, Jed had never really considered it before. He wondered if there was a partner about, but he had never really seen her with a man or a woman, for that matter. Probably, she was just too busy. Still, it was a shame there wasn't someone to enjoy her delicious baking.

'So, how long have you been here?'

'Oh, about three years. I was a professional show jumper before that. Used to compete at all the big events, but retired a couple of horses, so decided to get into racing.

Jed was surprised. From the look of the place, it was almost as if she had just moved in.

'What level did you compete at?' Jed couldn't help asking as he had friends who used to do the circuits.

Lydia smiled. 'Oh, all the BSJA events, you know.'

Jed nodded. Well, that explained her prowess at schooling. The British Show Jumping Association classes events were graded in terms of difficulty. She was probably very good. He made a mental note to look her up as all the results were online these days.

'Well, just stick with it. It's great to ride horses that have been schooled to jump properly. It makes a real difference.'

Lydia nodded, clearly pleased. 'Hey, talking of my horses, several of whom were ridden by Eddie, how is he doing? I called in at the hospital to see him. Will he recover do you think?'

It was a question Jed had asked himself repeatedly. 'I think so, bloody hope so anyway. They can do amazing things these days.'

'Do they know how it happened?

'The police are looking into it. The theory is he passed out from dehydration.'

Lydia raised an eyebrow at that. 'Well, he did struggle with his weight, but you don't believe that?'

Jed shrugged. It would be so easy to confide in Lydia, but if he was wrong it would be so damaging for Eddie. Supposing, he recovered only to find that all his rides had dried up because of rumours and speculation? That was why he had chosen Imogen to help him because she had no association with the sport at all. He could perhaps ask some other questions though.

'Yeah. I guess it was just an accident.' Jed suddenly thought of something. 'Still, his girlfriend, Felicity Hill, has wasted no time and seems to have turned her attentions to Jake Horton. You should have heard him going on about some party he went to with her over the weekend. He's even off to Henry Winter's birthday party in a couple of weeks. I hope it wasn't serious between Eddie and Felicity or else he's going to be devastated.'

Lydia looked thoughtful. 'Poor Eddie. I must say I was rather surprised at her appointment. What do you make of her?'

'Well, I liked old Penny and at least she knew her stuff. Let's hope Felicity is a fast learner because she doesn't know one end of a horse from another.'

'I suppose she was appointed just for her looks,' Lydia suggested.

'Mmm, I'd certainly like to know how she was appointed. She certainly isn't the sort of person you would put forward for the role. She looks like she should work behind a makeup counter.'

Jed knew he preferred a more natural look, but from the comments from the lads, he could see that Felicity might be popular with a certain type of audience. He decided to change the subject.

'Listen. I'm riding for your neighbour too. Hugh Mitchell. What's he like?'

Lydia shrugged. 'I know he's only over there.' She pointed through the window to the house in the distance. 'We share some gallops and stuff, but I hardly ever see him, actually. I have met Anton du Pre once.'

Jed nodded, thinking that it was rather strange that they didn't communicate more. It might actually be quite helpful to share information and resources.

'OK. Not to worry, I'll see him tomorrow probably. So, I suppose you get to hear all sorts set as you are in the heart of Walton.'

It was a clumsy attempt to get Lydia to open up, but instead she gave him a strange look.

'Not about Hugh Mitchell anyway, he keeps himself to himself. And as for Eddie, well he's everyone's favourite Irish jockey so I'm keeping everything crossed. Do you think it was an accident, what with the police investigating, is that purely routine?'

'I think so. The police know what they're doing, of course.'

Lydia nodded. 'I saw Geraldine McLoughlin at the hospital, you know, Kieran's wife. She looked pretty cut up. Penny Morris, you know, the old presenter was there too.'

That didn't surprise him. 'Good old Penny. Anyone else?'

'Yeah, Gary McKay was just coming out. He looked really cut up.'

So, it was Gary. Now, that was a shock given the fact that there was no love lost between them. What was Gary doing there?

'Wow, that's a turn up for the books, given the fact that Eddie took Gary's job as stable jockey.'

Lydia shrugged. 'Well, I think that Eddie was always an immense talent, and, in the end, he was bound to get taken on as a stable jockey.' Lydia's face fell. 'God, it must be so awful for Eddie's family, it really must. Have they come over from Ireland?'

'Oh, yes. Eddie's mother came over almost immediately, I'm surprised you didn't meet her actually. She is staying with me now. I'm in York and she can visit the hospital quite easily, whereas if she stayed at Eddie's she would need transport.'

Lydia beamed. 'Oh, that's so kind of you, Jed. You really are a brick, and a very good friend to Eddie.'

Jed flushed. 'Well, it's the least I can do. We jockeys must stick together, of course.'

Lydia took another bite of the cake. 'Indeed, you must. Now, what do you think about entries for Just A minute?' She turned on her laptop. 'There's a decent race at Wetherby only it's in better company and it's a bit of a longer race than his last outing. What do you think?'

Jed turned his attention to the challenging task of matching horses to races, reflecting on the fact that Lydia had confirmed who Eddie's visitors were. He was certainly surprised about Gary McKay, but he wasn't at all sure that Gary wasn't still bearing a huge grudge against Eddie. In that case, what was he doing there? He decided to look more closely at the surly Scot.

It was late when he arrived back home. Bernadette heard the door and came rushing to greet him in her dressing gown, her eyes shining, her hair loose and her skin covered in face cream.

'Jed, Jed. The Lord has remembered me in his prayers, so he has.'

Jed calmed her down to hear the full story. It seemed that the swelling in Eddie's brain had begun to lessen, not sufficiently to attempt to revive him from the coma just yet, but it seemed the treatment was working, and it was an encouraging sign.

'Fabulous, really great. Would you a celebratory Scotch or whatever your tipple is?' It was excellent news. Jed poured the whiskey and Bernadette decided on a hot chocolate.

'Me da was a drinker and I swore I'd never go down that road,' she replied, eyeing his glass darkly. 'Now before I forget I've bought some food for that wee cat of Eddie's when you're next down that way.'

'Cat? I'd no idea he had a cat. I can't recall seeing any sign of it. Damn. I'd better go back and feed the thing. Do you suppose he has a cat flap?' Privately, he was really worried. Eddie had been in hospital for nearly two weeks now. He hoped that someone else had thought to feed him, a neighbour or something otherwise he wasn't holding out much hope that the animal would still be alive.

'Oh. Don't worry. I'd have mentioned it before, but my head was so full of Eddie and his accident. The animal is a hardy type, a proper country cat, probably a good mouser, so don't you worry.'

Jed knew he'd not be able to sleep a wink worrying about the wretched thing and put down his glass. He would just have to go and leave some food at least.

'Look. I'll pop back it's no bother. We can't have Eddie arriving home to find that his cat has starved to death. What sort it is and what's he or she called?'

Bernadette pulled out her phone and began tapping away on the keys and then passed it to him.

'There he is, he's a fine fellow, so he is. He's called Seamus.'

He squinted at the photos of a handsome mainly black cat with white paws and a white muzzle. Easy enough to identify.

Bernadette held out a plastic bag full of sachets of Whiskers.

'You're a grand chap. Oh, I nearly forgot there was a call from a young lady, Imogen?'

Jed nodded. He had already received a text from her. He'd ring her later. But for now, he had to feed bloody Seamus.

He drove as fast as he could. It was a moonless, inky black night and the roads were empty. When he arrived at Eddie's he took out his torch and shone it round the path that led to cottage hoping to find the creature.

'Here Seamus, where are you? Come on boy, I have food.' He heard a bird's wings flapping somewhere in the distance, as he fished out the key to the door. But he didn't need it. He snapped on the light blinking at its brightness as he took in the carnage. Someone had been there before him and had obviously been searching for something, as the contents of the kitchen drawers and cabinets were spewed out all over the floor. He walked through into the sitting room where cushions and chairs were turned on their side. He turned to climb the stairs and out of the gloom, a figure rushed towards him wielding something. Then, the something was smashed into his skull, he felt a searing pain, and everything became dark.

Sometime later, Jed staggered to his feet and rubbed his sore head. He took in his surroundings and went outside to see if there was any sign of his attacker. He dimly remembered a dark figure of average build, whack him over the head before rushing off. He found his torch and peered into the darkness. The street was quiet, and it was clear that whoever had broken in had got clean away. He heard a rustle of leaves at one side of him and something wound itself around his legs and miaowed. Seamus, he presumed. He stroked the cat and searched through the chaos to find a saucer. Seamus gobbled his food greedily.

He tried to tidy up as best he could, found a cat flap in the rear door and left an enormous pile of cat biscuits in another bowl and a saucer of water. Seamus looked at him scornfully. He was clearly not a biscuit fan and he guessed that Bernadette's assessment of Seamus was correct. There, that would have to do for now. He wondered what on earth his assailant was searching for and who he was.

He looked on his phone for a security firm who could board up the house out of hours, when he found a neighbour hovering outside the door. She looked anxious and a little suspicious. She was a young woman of about twenty five with large eyes and a diffident manner.

'Hello, can I help you?'

'Hi, I live next door. I feed Seamus for Eddie when he's away. I heard about the accident, so I can feed him until he comes back.' She suddenly looked upset. 'He will get better, won't he?'

Jed nodded. 'I think so, but it's early days.' He suddenly thought he probably seemed very suspicious creeping around at night. He held out his hand. 'I'm Jed Cavendish a good friend of Eddie's. His mother is staying at mine whilst he's ill and she happened to mention that he had a cat. I came out to feed him, but someone had already broken in. Listen did you see or hear anything earlier? I'm just going to ring the police to let them know and get that door patched up.'

The woman shook her head. 'No, I had some music on earlier, so probably missed it. I work in the local pub, so know a lot of the lads. I recognise you from off the TV. Listen, why don't you come in whilst you ring the police?'

Jed did so, although the police were not particularly interested. He rang a security company who assured him they would visit that night and secure the property by boarding up the door. The woman, Lisa, noticing Jed yawning, said she would wait up and direct them to the damaged door so he could get home.

Jed was feeling very tired so was grateful to Lisa.

She smiled. 'It's no bother. I'm fond of Eddie. I used to get tips off him and the lads in the pub, so I hope he recovers.'

Jed could only nod in agreement. He suspected that she was more than a little fond of Eddie and wondered again about the women in his life. Perhaps she was one of them? Eddie could have a legion of female fans with his quick wit and ready charm, for all he knew. He glanced at his watch, saw the time and said his goodbyes.

As he went to his car, he noticed a something fluttering in the wind and managed to pick it up. It was a dirty business card, torn at one edge. It read- *LDF Horse Transport*. It listed an address in nearby

York and a phone number. Had his assailant dropped it? He wasn't sure, but he pocketed it anyway, his head hurting, not just from the blow, but from the uncomfortable thoughts swirling around his brain.

Chapter 14

Imogen was running late. She jogged down the road to the bar where she'd arranged to meet Jed, neatly stepping over puddles from the recent downpour and tried to banish the day's stresses. She had spent hours with a homesick first year student, who was considering jacking in her course in and going back home where her boyfriend was waiting. Several hours later, she had at least persuaded her to stay for the end of the month and arrange for the boyfriend to visit, but it had taken much longer than she had anticipated. Then, she'd had a couple of students worrying that they had taken the wrong course and had to advise them on their options.

Jed was already at 'The Nag's Head' looking rather gorgeous in a well cut grey suit, white shirt and a smart gold watch flashing at his wrist. Expensive, Imogen decided. She noticed that his shirt also looked luxurious, the sort with proper cuffs which were fastened together by horse head cufflinks. Not for the first time she wondered about his background and decided he was seriously posh. He kissed her cheeks, leaving her blushing and went off to the bar to buy her a drink. She was bursting to tell him her findings and was about to when he announced.

'Well, I have good news about Eddie, Bernadette tells me his latest brain scan shows the swelling is reducing. It's too early for him to come out of his coma just yet, but a definite improvement. Then Bernadette told me she has bought some cat food for his cat! I never even knew he had one, so I went there last night to feed the thing and found the place had been broken into and turned over. And the intruder was still in the house and hit me over the head. Look.' Jed turned his head to show her where there were cuts and abrasions on the side of his head. 'I rang the police who came but they think it was an opportunist who knew Eddie was still in hospital. But I'm sure someone was searching for something very particular. I wonder what?'

Imogen's brain was in overdrive. 'Did you get a good look at the person?'

Jed shook his head. 'No, they came down the stairs from the shadows. I didn't see anything really. It all happened so quickly. Still nothing major was stolen, so it was no ordinary burglary, they definitely were looking for something specific.'

'I think I have a good idea what.' She fished into her bag and handed the photo over to Jed. 'I presume that the man is Eddie, but who is she?'

Jed looked at her open mouthed. 'Where did you find this?'

'It was in the bank statements and there's something more. Having studied his accounts in more depth, it is clear that over the past six months Eddie has definitely had another source of income. He's been able to save about twelve grand or so and has barely spent any of his wages which suggests that he has been living on his bribes. My guess is that his bribes were paid in cash and he used the money to pay for essentials, in effect laundering it and then was able to save his wages.'

'Wow, you have been busy.' He studied the photo again. 'Well, that looks like Eddie from the back and it's definitely the front window of his house, I'd know that creeper anywhere.' He studied the photo. 'That ring too, I've definitely seen Eddie wear it, it's a family heirloom, a Claddagh ring or something.' He pored over the photo. 'But the woman, she looks familiar too.' His face dropped as realisation dawned. 'God, that would explain things. It's Geraldine.'

'Who?'

118

Jed lowered his voice. 'Bloody Geraldine McLoughlin, only Kieran McLoughlin's wife. I think there's a photo of her at Eddie's too. Looks to me like they were more than just employer's wife and employee.' Jed abstractly ran his fingers through his hair, waiting for Imogen to make the connection. 'Eddie is Kieran's stable jockey, so it looks like he's been playing with fire by having an affair with the boss's wife. Now do you get it? It makes sense and Lydia Fox mentioned that Geraldine visited Eddie. She was distraught apparently.'

'Shit.'

Jed took a sip of wine. 'So, whoever is behind the scam has found this information out and used it to blackmail Eddie.'

Imogen took a deep breath. 'So that's why he moved out of the yard into his own place. More privacy. Listen. I think this thing could be bigger than we think. I haven't told you about my brother, have I?'

Jed looked confused. 'No, what about your brother?'

Imogen blurted out the whole story. Jed listened carefully, and his fingers reached across the table to touch hers when she described the injury she had received when she was attacked by men mistaking her for her brother.

'I was wearing his hoodie, you see, and one of the guys had a knife. They were trying to collect drug debts from Marcus and realised their mistake, but only after I'd received this.' Imogen pulled down her the top of her dress to reveal the jagged scar beneath her collar bone.

Jed whistled. 'That's awful, Imogen. I'm so sorry. But what does this have to do with Eddie?'

'I was coming to that. You see my mother and I visit Marcus in prison every week. He's inside for drug dealing. My mother is always thinking of jobs he could do when he comes out and he mentioned he fancied a career as a professional gambler. He had been betting inside prison and been quite lucky as some of the other cons had told him about a betting system they use. Then he said that he would have won more if it wasn't for the sixth race at Uttoxeter. You see, *twelve in the sixth.* It all makes sense. He bet on another horse to win in the sixth race because he knew Eddie wasn't supposed to win that race.'

Jed took another sip of wine. 'I suppose it could be a coincidence?'

Imogen shook her head. 'No. I told him about Eddie's accident, just mentioned it in passing and he said all the right things, but I knew he was hiding something. He's my little brother and I always know when he's done something or is lying. It's some sixth sense, I suppose. And I think he knows that the accident was payback because Eddie didn't do as he was told.'

Jed looked thoughtful. 'So, do you think your brother is directly involved?'

'No, but someone in the prison knows something and it's been passed onto the others. So, whoever the Mr Big is, he has links with the criminal fraternity.'

'Jesus.'

Imogen fished out a notebook and started to make some notes.

'Right. Let's write down everything we know; all the facts and we'll take it from there.'

Jed nodded. I'll get another round in. I think.' He paused. 'Another thing, I have looked at the other six races and the results were rather interesting.'

Several drinks later Imogen had nearly filled her notebook.

'So, four out of the other six races looked dodgy… Are you sure?'

Jed nodded miserably. 'Well, I have studied them several times and Eddie does not seem to be giving it his best effort.' Jed was clearly struggling with it. 'It's subtle, but a furlong out or so he has made stupid errors with positioning in one race, appears to be holding the horse back too much so he can't make up the ground up in another, has a fall that he should have been able to sit and in another he is using his leg, but holding the horse up at the same time. It's not really obvious, but I'm not convinced the horses were given their best chance. In all the races Hugh Mitchell's horses profited in the end.'

'Right.' Imogen took this in. 'So, Hugh Mitchell is definitely worth taking a closer look at.'

'Yes, I'd say so. The horses that won were about fifth or sixth favourites, not rank outsiders, but with long enough odds to be worth betting on without raising any suspicion. But racing is so unpredictable, I'm not sure how they could be certain that Hugh's horses would win, certain enough to risk betting heavily. There must be more to it.'

Imogen sighed. Just when she thought they were getting somewhere, Jed had to throw in another curve ball.

'OK. Well, at least that's a start. I think it would be a good idea to study those races and look at patterns, there must be some reason why those races and those horses were chosen.'

'I suppose you could just ask your brother what he knows?'

Imogen was appalled. 'What? He'd be a sitting duck passing information on about a scam. He could be attacked and he's due out on licence soon. No, we just have to think logically and sensibly about this.'

'No, you're quite right. Sorry.' Jed squeezed her hand. 'I wasn't thinking straight.'

Imogen relaxed. 'It's OK. Now who else knows about Geraldine and Eddie? We're looking for someone inside the industry who knows stuff about people and is prepared to use it against them. Someone was desperate to get that photo back. Do you think the affair is still going on? I mean wasn't that woman from the racing programme going out with him, what's her name Felicity someone?'

'Well, I think she has turned her attention to another jockey now, Jake Horton and it was probably just a flirtation thing with Eddie, especially if he was otherwise involved. Jake was going on about some party he'd taken her to, so I suppose she's with him now. Interesting that Geraldine had visited so often. She must be so worried.'

'Enough to talk to us, do you think?'

'I doubt it. She has too much to lose. Kieran would go absolutely nuts. Still, she may know who was blackmailing Eddie, he's likely to have said something.'

Jed nodded thoughtfully. 'But be very careful what you say to people and watch yourself. In fact, say absolutely nothing to anyone about what we are investigating. We could be dealing with some pretty violent types. I mean, look what happened to me.'

Imogen nodded. 'Of course, fine, but listen do you think the intruder knows you're onto them? Would they have recognised you?'

Jed thought for a while. 'Maybe. Whoever was in the house might just think I was there to feed Eddie's cat. So, don't worry. I did sort something out with the neighbour, so I won't need to keep going back and forth. It makes you think though, doesn't it? We need to be very careful.'

'Hey, I'm not worried. You're forgetting that I am a martial arts expert, aren't you? But I will be careful.'

Jed laughed. 'Oh yes, you said. You really are a surprising girl, you know that? Now if I'll suss out Hugh Mitchell's place and see if I can have a private chat with Geraldine.'

'You might be better catching her when she's visiting Eddie. That way she's more likely to be on her own.'

'Good thinking, and with Kieron being so busy now the season's in full swing, he wouldn't have the time. Perhaps, Bernadette can text me when she turns up next, I'll ask her.'

They arranged to meet in a few days and stay in touch by text.

'Be vague just in case our phones are stolen, or something. We don't want to give anything away.'

'OK.'

Imogen drove home, her spirits lifting. It had been great to get Marcus's story off her chest. Jed had been sympathetic and hadn't looked at her like she had two heads. He had taken her seriously, which was the main thing. Now, all she had to do was apply her brain to the facts. She liked nothing better than a puzzle to solve. Besides, Jed had called her 'surprising' and she found she kept replaying the scene where he had said this, round and round. It wasn't as though she even liked him like that. But it was more that for the first time since Sam had departed she felt alive, with a renewed sense of purpose. Whether they were in danger or not and whatever the outcome, it felt wonderful.

It was only when Jed arrived back home that he realised he had forgotten to tell her about the *LDF Horse Transport* business card he had found. Still, it might not be important and probably had nothing to do with the intruder, after all, Eddie lived in an area where there were lots of racing yards and many of them may have dropped that card. He mulled over what Imogen had said about her brother. He felt curiously protective of her. Still, some of his school friends had experimented with harder drugs, progressing quickly from the odd joint that was a rite of passage for youngsters, and he had seen what it had done to people. But the link with the prison and the criminal fraternity was very worrying indeed. He had been quite cavalier when Imogen had asked him about whether his assailant realised who he was, but he decided he could probably get away with the cover story of helping Eddie out by feeding his cat. He was so glad that he had resisted the impulse to discuss the case with anyone inside racing. It was quite a closed community and speculation and rumour soon was reported as fact. They needed to redouble their efforts and quickly, especially as Eddie showed some sign of improvement. A cold finger of alarm inched down his spine when he realised that Eddie might be more at risk if and when he recovered and could talk to the police about what had happened to him. When he arrived home the house was still and dark, so Bernadette must be in bed. His head still felt rather sore, so he decided to have an early night himself and hoped that sleeping on things might make them that bit clearer.

Chapter 15

Before Jed made his way to Hugh Mitchell's yard, he received a call from his agent, Lawrence Kent. Lawrence had rather a good reputation as an agent and Jed had been lucky to get him to take him on his books. He was a confident Yorkshire chap, always cheery and upbeat and today was no exception.

'So, how's it going lad?'

'Pretty good, actually. I'm picking up some good rides, could always do with a few more, of course.'

He heard the excitement in Lawrence's voice. 'Aye, well I've been hearing good reports about yer, you're getting out there, getting noticed, so much so Hugh Mitchell rang me asking if you'd pick up some rides for him. He's quite a small trainer, but it would get you known, lad.'

Jed smiled to himself. Lawrence's conversations were always peppered with phrases like 'get yourself out there' and 'put your best foot forward' and he was good at making contacts with trainers and pushing his jockeys. That was why he was excellent at his job, he supposed.

'Great. In fact, I'm one step ahead of you, Lawrence, I'm on my way there now to ride out, actually. I've already ridden for him actually.'

'Fantastic, lad, fantastic. His usual jockey has gone to earth, it seems, so he's keen to engage someone else and your name came up, so remember to make a good impression, lad, put your best foot forward. Not that I need to tell you, being out of the top drawer and all that.'

'No, but thanks anyway. I will be on my best behaviour, as I always am.'

'Great stuff, fantastic. You're still able to make the weights OK?'

'No problem there.'

'Great stuff. I'll leave you to it and remember best foot forward. Speak to you soon.'

Jed's spirits lifted as he called into Hugh Mitchell's stables. It was a day or so before he was due to ride for him but being engaged for more rides was really encouraging. He took in his surroundings. There was a small house and thirty or so stables, with more being constructed in the rear. The place was clean and tidy. He called at the house hoping to catch Hugh in. He had tried to research Hugh Mitchell beforehand, but there was limited information, a website which wasn't up to date and a few grainy pictures of a smallish man with his collar up, wearing a trilby. He could be aged anything from thirty to fifty and Jed felt obscurely disappointed that the image was so poor. He was clearly a man who avoided the limelight. Due to his slight stature, Jed wondered if he had been a former jockey but although his website boasted a keen interest in horses from an early age, there was nothing to suggest that he had been. He was disappointed again when there was no answer at the door and instead his assistant trainer, Anton Du Pre appeared from the yard and motioned for him to follow him.

'Mr Mitchell not in?'

'No. He away. You ride grey?'

There was a string about to go out with six horses and riders. Anton muttered something to the riders, and they eyed Jed whilst they waited for him to tack up the grey Periwinkle and go with them. He was riding Nomad in a couple of days but clearly Anton was saving the horse's energy for that race. He spotted Spooks and Top of the Morning, a bay and a chestnut, the horses that had both won when he suspected Eddie had pulled the favourites.

The work riders looked to be stable hands and there were at least two girls who were gossiping behind their hands and eyeing Jed appreciatively. He smiled his most charming smile and vaulted into the saddle, as the group made their way to the gallops. The stables were in Market Leighton and backed onto Lydia Fox's paddocks at their furthermost point. As they rode he was at the rear whilst the two girls were just up ahead with Anton leading the way on a bay horse. Jed rode on catching up with the next horse, so he could speak to the rider, a pretty blonde.

'What's it like working here. Mr Mitchell, OK is he?'

She smiled. 'Well, Anton runs the place really. It's alright. A job at least.'

Jed nodded. 'You've had some good winners, with good odds.'

The girl looked at him warily as Anton reined his horse in to wait for them. Anton gave her sharp look. The girl looked down and kicked on. Clearly, Anton did not like their discussion which made him think that he could understand a lot more English than he had let on.

They passed a shipping container situated towards the rear of the land which was obscured by a row of conifers. Jed noticed a very heavy-duty lock on the side panel and wondered what on earth was in it to require such robust security. Probably, hurdles or other equipment to make jumps out of or perhaps something more sinister? Definitely worth investigating, he decided. When they arrived at the gallops, Anton turned his horse round to face them.

'Three circuits,' he raised his hand to show his three middle fingers. 'You go.'

The gallops were well maintained and all weather. Jed followed the others with Periwinkle enjoying the pace. His horse showed good speed initially but began to tire on the third and final circuit. He pushed a little further and realised that the horse had little left to give so allowed him to drop back. He noticed a full range of jump hurdles in the small paddock adjoining and hoped to be able to let Periwinkle catch his breath and then school him over the hurdles. From what he recalled, the horse certainly needed it.

Fortunately, Anton seemed to agree, and they took it in turns to canter round and jump the hurdles. Periwinkle jumped reasonably well on his own, but mindful of his experience on the racecourse, Jed managed to get Periwinkle to jump alongside another horse, albeit several feet away. On the next round he moved his mount nearer to the other horse and kept his leg firmly pressed on his mount's left side and used his right rein to prevent Periwinkle from shying away. Once satisfied that Periwinkle had learned not to jump away, he tightened his reins and drew him to a halt.

Anton nodded to him. 'Better, I think.'

'Yes. I just wanted him to learn to jump near other horses.'

Anton grinned and nodded. At least despite the language barrier, they had similar training objectives which was something. As they rode back to the yard, Jed tried to engage the blonde stable girl in conversation again. He wondered what his mount, Nomad, was like.

'I look after him. He's lovely, a real softie.'

'Does he have a chance of winning?'

'Yeah, I'd say so. His stamina has really improved. I expect he'll have decent odds.'

'Who normally rides for you?'

'Well, we've had Gary McKay a lot recently.' The blonde looked for Anton, making sure he was out of earshot. 'Perhaps, you'll be our regular jockey now?'

There was no mistaking the flirtatious hair flicking motion even under her helmet. She clearly considered that he was a much better option than the surly Scot. Then what she had just said exploded into his consciousness. Gary McKay. What Lawrence said about Hugh Mitchell's usual jockey going to ground, reverberated round his brain. What had happened to Gary?

His mind racing, Jed smiled back, but he had no wish to pursue her. There were more important matters to hand.

As they hacked back to the yard, they passed the shipping container again. From this approach it was clear that there was a well worn path towards it, which was worn enough to suggest very regular use. He wondered what the hell was in the container. It must be something very valuable. He vowed to gain entry and have a better look.

As they came by the house, Jed noticed someone or something. There was a shadow passing by the window.

'So, I take it Mr Mitchell is back? I would like to meet him, if I may.'

Anton smiled, but his eyes were cold. 'No. Is cleaner. I tell you Mr Mitchell is away.' There was a hard edge to his voice. Jed wasn't at all sure he believed him. He was certain he was hiding something and that something was related to Hugh Mitchell.

Jed loved Market Rasen racecourse. Nestled within the Lincolnshire Wolds, the place had a rural charm all of its own and his spirits lifted as he drove through the countryside. Besides riding Nomad in the third, he was riding for Lydia and had a couple of rides of Kieran McLoughlin. In the weighing room, although some of the lads asked about Eddie, Jed realised that his accident was becoming a distant memory and people were moving on with their lives. Besides they now had another juicy piece of gossip to discuss. What had happened to Gary McKay? There were various theories.

'I heard he went off after a row with his missus or something,' suggested Tristan Davies.

'Or got beaten up for annoying someone he shouldn't have. He is a miserable so and so,' replied Gavin Shearing.

Jed didn't even know he had a wife and felt ashamed that he had never even considered it. Yet there was something about Gary and his abrasive nature, that did not invite confidences or endear him to people.

'Still it's an ill wind,' replied Tristan. 'I wonder who will get his rides?'

Jed felt rather uncomfortable at this. 'Well, my agent rang and looks like I'll be getting some of them at least. Still it makes you wonder, doesn't it? Do you think it's anything to do with what happened to Eddie?'

Tristan looked shocked. 'No, why would it be? You know Gary, he's probably gone off in a strop or something. I'm sure he'll turn up fine.'

It was such a burden, thought Jed, knowing what had happened to Eddie and not being able to share this with anyone apart from Imogen. Was Gary's disappearance linked to what had happened to Eddie? Still, everyone else seemed blissfully unaware and were carrying on as normal. He would be too, if he hadn't picked up

Eddie's bloody phone and heard that stupid message. Gary's disappearance had to be related, surely?

'Do you think someone has contacted the police about Gary? You know, to report him missing...'

Tristan clapped his back with a smile. 'Look, you know what's he like. I'm sure he'll surface. He has had a bit of a drink problem in the past, so he's probably lying pissed somewhere, that's all. Just make the most of getting his rides, that's my advice.' Still it was hard to shake off the terrible feeling of foreboding Jed had. Was Gary THE brains behind the scam or had he met with an accident? Perhaps, he was feeling the wrath of whoever was behind the scam too?

He tuned into the hum of the conversation in the weighing room. People had moved on and were listening to something else. The lads were listening to Jake telling them about a swanky party he had been to with Felicity which loads of celebs had attended. Several models, lots of TV presenters and rock stars were on the guest list, including some well known captains of industry.

'It was bloody brilliant mate. Felicity knows everyone. I had a drink with ex England footballer, David Kerr, got chatting with him and some of his mates are interested in buying racehorses, so I was able to advise them where to buy, the best trainers and jockeys, of course.' There was a ripple of laughter. Jake's relationship with Felicity could give his career a very welcome boost. 'And I'm off to Lord Winter's party with her in a week or so. I'm going up in the world and no mistake.'

Tristan Davies caught Jed's eye. Jed knew Henry Winter rather well, in fact, he was Arabella's brother and his own invitation to the birthday bash had arrived only last week. Still he had no intention of going as Arabella was bound to be there and he really didn't want to encourage her. Tristan gave him a conspiratorial nudge.

'It's all well and good now, but what happens when it all goes tits up? Felicity doesn't strike me as someone who will stick around a guy for long. There will always be someone richer, more good looking, with more influence...'

'Know what you mean,' replied Jed. 'He's happy, I guess.' Still, it was interesting that Tristan, who never had a bad word to say about anyone, was concerned about Jake.

'Yeah. He's like a dog with two tails, for now...' The words hung ominously between them.

In the end he had a reasonable day. Lydia's horse, Ragamuffin, came in fourth. Lydia was delighted and beamed as usual. He rode two of Kieron McLoughlin's horses, one of whom ran down the field and the other who pecked on landing, sending Jed over his mount's head. Fortunately, he avoided being trampled on and was a little stiff but fit enough to take up his ride in the last race. Hugh Mitchell's horse, Nomad, who had little previous form, was way out in the betting but came in a close second to Jake Horton's mount, Brandy Snap, the red-hot favourite. Jed had wondered if Hugh would put in an appearance, but as usual it was Anton who officiated and gave him his bewilderingly brief instructions, 'just run.'

Nonetheless, Jake's win gave him the opportunity to see him and his girlfriend at close range, as Felicity interviewed him. As usual she was dressed in figure hugging clothes, with riding boots, a mini skirt showing a large expanse of taut thigh and a tight tweed jacket. Her nails were long and red, and she had such long false eyelashes, it almost looked like she had spiders attached to her eyelids. Her hair was worn loose, and she flicked her shiny tresses at regular intervals, as if she was in a shampoo commercial. Even from a distance he was almost asphyxiated by clouds of the perfume 'Poison'. Felicity kept clutching at Jake's arm, and he gazed back at her, clearly absolutely smitten. During the interview he heard Jake patiently explain that his horse, Brandy Snap, was a bright *chestnut* colour rather than *ginger* as she described him. Felicity nodded and smiled, unfazed by her latest faux pas. Perhaps, at least she would actually learn something about bloody horses from her relationship with Jake, which had to be a good thing. However, he tended to share Tristan's view that they would be left to pick up the pieces of Jake's shattered heart when she moved on. Even though he was just a disinterested bystander, he felt uneasy on Jake's behalf. A bruising break-up was as inevitable as diets followed the excesses of Christmas, but sadly Jake was too head over heels to see it coming.

As he was leaving, he bumped into Penny Morris. She was wearing her customary old quilted jacket and tweed skirt. Her grey hair was pulled back by an Alice band which gave her a rather severe look.

'Now then Jed. Well ridden. Did you hear that stupid girl describe Brandy Snap as 'ginger'? For goodness sake!'

Jed patted her arm kindly. 'I know, Penny. And for what it's worth I don't think she's a patch on you. I never got the chance to say how sorry I was about what happened.'

Penny smiled, a little mollified. 'You always were a dear boy. It happens to women of a certain age in television and I've had a good career, so I'm really not bitter. There's just something about her I'm not sure of.' A look of distaste crossed her face. 'Racing people all know each other, but she came from nowhere. Who exactly is she? I just don't trust her, somehow and it's not just sour grapes.' Penny seemed about to say more but changed her mind. 'Anyway, how is Eddie? I was shocked to hear about his accident, even more so when I saw him. Such a lovely boy. Mind you that Felicity got her claws into him too. Just watch out she'll be on the lookout for another jockey now he's off the scene.'

Jed nodded. He was tempted to tell her about Jake but decided against it. He tried to steer the conversation onto more neutral topics.

As he said his goodbyes, he reflected on the fact that Penny really needed something else to think about other than bloody Felicity Hill. Penny was right, she had appeared from nowhere. He pondered on her suspicions. He had thought of Felicity as relatively harmless. Was he missing something?

Chapter 16

Imogen was going through questionnaires and inputting data into the computer. She found, though, that she was increasingly distracted from her work about the effect of statins to thinking about Eddie, Jed and the racing scam. She found herself checking the racing results and eager for titbits of information about the racing world. She also spent some time picking over the information. In her work she was accustomed to looking for patterns and themes and considering the facts behind them. She was convinced that patient, analytical thought would help her consider the facts, look objectively at the likely causes and draw sensible conclusions which should lead to them to find out who was the brains behind the operation. Another nagging thought was what Marcus knew about the betting system and how she could exploit his knowledge without placing him at risk. He was due out on licence within a couple of months and she desperately didn't want to jeopardise this. Yet instinctively she knew that Marcus knew something about Eddie's 'accident' and the reasons behind it. She pondered on this and decided that it might be a good idea to speak to his probation officer or be present when her mother spoke to him and express their worries about him getting into gambling. After all, weren't they obliged to check out Marcus's support networks before he was released to his mother's address and suggest suitable employment? Perhaps, they might also let slip who else was currently within HMP Hull who would know about the scam? Marcus words echoed round her head. *I would have won much more if it wasn't for the last race at Uttoxeter.* He must have been talking about the same race that Eddie won. Someone in the prison knew something, that much was for sure.

Idly, Imogen searched for stories about criminals who were brought to justice, crooked bookmakers, jockeys, trainers, anyone involved in racing who could be involved. She found nothing of interest and gave up as she had no idea what she was looking for anyway. Sighing, she listed each horse that Jed agreed Eddie had pulled and tried to research owners, trainers, breeders, racecourses, even distances to see if there were any patterns in the information. At a loss, she googled racing personalities and came across an article about Felicity Hill. She had heard Jed talk about her and read on with interest. She was rather surprised at the presenter's model girl looks which had rather a hard edge to them. Just too much fake tan, makeup and lashings of mascara, Imogen decided. The article explained that Felicity had been something of a glamour model turned 'it' girl and had decided to try her hand at TV presenting. It also mentioned her 'rock', her father, who had an abiding love of horseracing and had inspired her to try out for the presenter's job for the programme. She also gave thanks to her agent Liam Sawyer who had also supported her even though Felicity herself had doubts about her own ability.

'I've always loved horses, adored the racing scene, the glamour and glitz,' Felicity added, but she admitted that she had found it hard at first and struggled with the terminology. She was apparently keen to silence her critics and stated that she was a 'quick learner' and knew she had 'made some mistakes.' That was something of an understatement if Jed's comments were anything to go by. But most of all she stated that she admired the jockeys enormously.

'The boys are bloody amazing and super helpful as well as brave. I love them all,' she added.

Given her relationships with at least two of the jockeys, Imogen hoped this was more of a figure of speech than a declaration of intention. Finally, Felicity stated that she hoped to introduce racing to a whole new audience and encourage young women to enjoy the races and not be put off by the terminology and macho betting culture. It all sounded quite plausible. Imogen wondered what Jed would make of the article and decided to bookmark it to show him. Yet the jury was still out it seemed if any of the comments from readers was to go by. Some listed her 'gaffes' and found them unforgivable whilst others found her 'easy on the eye' and a welcome change from some of the other older female presenters who were viewed as 'too county' and 'mumsy.' Others found her description of 'geldings' as 'boys without the toys' hysterically funny and 'refreshingly honest.' Imogen suspected the positive comments were mainly from men, but what was clear was that love Felicity or hate her, she had certainly generated interest in racing and viewing figures for the programme were very promising. It was an entertaining read and Imogen found herself writing down some of Felicity's quotes and the name of her agent for the sake of completeness. She was interrupted by Jack entering the room. She tried to close down the page, but not before he had caught sight of the online racing calendar.

'Fancy a sandwich for lunch? You look very hard at it, I'm sure you need a break.'

Imogen quickly flicked her computer back to her data pages and guiltily abandoned her search for the day. Honestly, she was becoming obsessed with this investigation, she decided, vowing to do some proper work when she came back afterwards. As she and Jack sat sipping mochas and eating toasted sandwiches in the student café, she tried to concentrate on what Jack was saying.

'Are you OK? You seem a little distracted. Not man trouble, I hope?'

Imogen shrugged. 'No, no…'

Jack studied her. 'Have you seen anything of Milly's brother?' His tone was light, but she wasn't fooled. Damn. He had definitely seen the racing page she was searching online. She decided to answer neutrally.

'Yes. As a friend. I'm quite interested in the racing actually.'

Jack paused then his face split into a huge grin. 'I get it. There's no need to feel ashamed. You want to know about racing as a way of trying to impress Jed, that's it, isn't it?'

Imogen was too stunned to speak. How could he have got everything so wrong, but better than telling him the truth she supposed. Jed had been quite clear that she should be tight lipped about their concerns. They had to be very careful what they said to anyone. Imogen sighed, unsure what to say next.

Jack beamed clearly taking her silence as agreement.

'Well, that's what girls do if they like someone. Milly suddenly became interested in Liverpool FC when she realised that I had been a lifelong supporter.' He took a sip of mocha. 'Hey, I can help. My dad fancies himself as a bit of a racing fan, national hunt particularly.' His face spread into a wide grin. 'Why don't I introduce you to him and he can give you some advice about racing then you can impress Jed? Good idea?'

Imogen opened her mouth to protest. 'Hmm, I was just interested in where Jed was racing next. That's all. Honestly.'

Jack gave her a cynical look. 'Look. I won't tell Milly, if that's what you're worried about. Your secret is safe with me.'

Whatever she said he still wasn't going to believe her, but she could hardly tell him about Eddie and the investigation that she and Jed were involved in. Great. Not only was she squirming with embarrassment because Jack had caught her googling the racing pages and thought she fancied Jed, she had to meet Jack's father and listen to him droning on and on about racing and she still hadn't found out anything that might be useful to their inquiries. At this rate Jed was going to regret getting her involved at all. She felt quite despondent, as though she was letting the side down. Still, she knew the value of hard work and vowed to redouble her efforts. After all, as well as helping Eddie, she would be able to prevent Marcus getting involved in anything illegal. Just then her mobile rang, and she answered it, glad of the distraction from Jack's knowing expression. She could hardly make out who it was, the voice was so racked by sobs. Imogen felt alarm jolt through her.

'Mum? Mum, is that you?'

'It's Marcus…Oh my God… he's been assaulted.'

Chapter 17

Bernadette had hoovered and cleaned his entire house, Jed noticed when he came in. Although the house looked tidy, he was disappointed that she had gone out as he had hoped to catch her to ask about Eddie's love life. He was feeling a little stuck about the investigation, if he was honest, and horribly guilty. He was plagued with worries about Gary McKay and hoped that he would turn up. Again, and again he wished that he had never picked up Eddie's phone. If he hadn't he would be ignorant of what Eddie was up to, Eddie would not be in a coma and quite possibly Gary would still be around scowling and putting a dampener on the usually buoyant mood in the weighing room. He completed some google searches, managed to find an address for Gary McKay and vowed to go there later. There had been nothing in the press about Gary's disappearance, so perhaps he had turned up again? He hoped to have something to useful to contribute when he met up with Imogen tomorrow.

Again, he found his thoughts twisted up in knots as he pondered on Eddie's relationship with Geraldine McLoughlin and Felicity. Was Eddie something of a ladies' man and seeing both women? Maybe Eddie had jettisoned Geraldine in favour of Felicity? Bernadette must have inkling he decided, as Irish mammies were pretty astute when it came to their offspring. She had left a note stating he was at the at the hospital, so Jed decided to follow her, see Eddie and do a bit of digging. He reckoned that Bernadette would also have a good idea by now which people were regular visitors to Eddie's bedside, and he wondered if Geraldine might be one of those in regular attendance.

Jed paused to buy some chocolates in the foyer of the Infirmary. He knew Eddie wouldn't be able to make much use of them at the moment, but at least it might be nice for Bernadette. As a 'thank you' for all her cleaning. He had explained that she really shouldn't feel obliged to do the housework, but she had replied that it helped keep her occupied and helped dispel any gloomy thoughts, so who was he to argue?

The corridors were shiny and smelt vaguely of disinfectant and polish. It was late afternoon and the place was still humming with activity, as visitors, nurses and porters scurried this way and that. He made his way into Eddie's room, where Bernadette was clutching his hand and talking to him in a low voice. She turned around and smiled as Jed came in.

'I'm just telling me lad about all the folks at home in Ballymena and reading the cards to him.' Jed noticed she had a pile of 'Get Well' cards and was systematically going through them. 'Look, Father Quigley is praying for you, Sinead from the shop and yer Uncle Sean.'

Jed pulled up a chair noticing that Eddie's hair had grown, his bruising had faded, but he was still supported by the machines which fed in his vital signs to computer monitors.

'So, any news? Look, I bought these for you.' He passed the expensive looking box of chocolates onto her.

Bernadette beamed. 'Oh, you shouldn't have. But no. Not since the last scan. We just have to keep hoping and praying. I'm sure he'll pull through with Father Quigley and the whole diocese praying for him.'

Jed felt rather touched by Bernadette's blind faith. He was not especially religious but could see how it would be very comforting at a time like this. He pulled up a chair opposite Bernadette and took Eddie's other hand in his. It felt warm and slightly clammy to the touch which he supposed was a good thing. At least he wasn't stone cold. He looked at the sweep of Eddie's dark lashes and the purple shadows beneath his eyes and wondered what on earth he would do if Eddie didn't make it? What Bernadette would do? He couldn't bear to think about that and felt his throat tighten. Yet time was moving on. He noticed the flowers in the room had all been changed, as they wilted and died. Even Eddie's fingernails had grown. A horrible thought flitted through his brain. If the intention of the attacker was to kill Eddie, then if he recovered, he might be in even greater danger. In fact, whoever was behind the attack might come back and finish the job. Yet, Jed was painfully aware that he had no hard evidence that he would use to persuade the police to put a watch on Eddie. He had to redouble his efforts to find out who was behind the betting scam and the attack soon, yet he felt despondent that so far, all their leads at fizzled out into nothing. So what if Hugh Mitchell was reclusive and had locked shipping container on his yard? It could all be entirely innocent, as could Gary McKay's disappearance. He was aware that Bernadette was continuing to read through the cards. There seemed to be loads of them. He listened at the lengthy list of familiar racing figures who had all been in touch until she had read them all.

'Well, he's certainly a very popular man back home and here of course. Has he had many visitors here, do you know?'

Bernadette's blue eyes twinkled. 'He has. Lots of jockeys, one or two girls, you know…'

Jed kept his tone light. 'Girls? Did Eddie have a particular girlfriend only he never said much to me or the lads. Kept his cards close to his chest, I suppose.'

Bernadette nodded.

'Aye, he was always a popular lad. He had a girlfriend from back home, Orla, but that fizzled out when he rode over here. I think there was someone though, 'cos he seemed happier, content, you know.'

'Did he mention a name only I would think she'd be desperately worried? Perhaps, she has visited, made herself known to you? Perhaps even send a card?'

Bernadette looked thoughtful. 'Well, right enough that nice Geraldine has visited with her husband Kieran and sat with him, oh, five or six times and then a couple of the lads have brought their girlfriends and as I was arriving that brassy one, who is on the TV, Felicity something, was just leaving. I remember 'cos the press were outside. She walks past me without a word and as she goes through the doors outside, the whole street was lit up with flash bulbs, so it was.'

Jed took this in, thinking that for Felicity it was probably a welcome photo opportunity. Perhaps that was all?

Bernadette frowned as she handed him the pile of cards.

'Look at them. It's a comfort to know that he is loved. It means so much…' She began dabbing at her eyes with a handkerchief.

Jed watched her, feeling rather helpless, as she fought back tears. Her phone rang and she stood up to take the call.

Jed squeezed Eddie's hand and looked at the familiar face. He looked as though he was just dozing and might wake up at any time.

'Come on mate. You can make it. Remember me and you fighting in out at the finish. Whatever you're involved in, we can sort it out.' He wished he could see into Eddie's head and find some sort of clue. He flicked through the cards. The whole racing community had pulled together, and it seemed that nearly every single trainer and jockey had signed them, with various messages. Charlie Durrant had added;

It's a hell of a way to get out of paying me back that tenner you owe me! Seriously though we miss your dulcet tones from the weighing room, so you'd better get back here quickly!

Eddie. You are a great friend and competitor. Have everything crossed you'll be back with us soon. Tristan

Miss you Eddie. Keeping your rides warm. Get well soon. Geraldine and Kieron xxxx

This had obviously been written by Geraldine if the line of kisses was anything to go by. Kisses certainly weren't Kieron's style, but then again, he didn't know if he should read anything into them. Lots of people used them liberally, especially women. He thought back to the photo Imogen had found which certainly seemed to suggest that Eddie and Geraldine were more than good friends. Still, she was hardly likely to advertise the fact in a card to Eddie that anyone could read. He really needed to see Geraldine on her own to question her about Eddie. He felt sure he would know by her expression if she was hiding something.

There were many more cards from other jockeys, owners and members of the public. Bernadette finished her call and sat down again, her face creased in anxiety. She looked on the verge of tears and so tired.

'Problem?'

'You could say. Eddie's sister, Siobhan, is about to give birth and I don't know who to be with, her or Eddie.' She wiped a tear from her eye. 'I want to be with them both, so I do. But I can't leave him,' she glanced at Eddie. 'Supposing he wakes up and I'm not here?'

Jed's mind was in overdrive. What an awful dilemma for her with both children needing her. There must be a solution.

'Look. Why don't you go, and I'll make sure that someone visits every day? I'll draw up a rota, maybe speak to Geraldine about it. Imogen would help and the lads too. And I'll get the hospital to ring me if there's any change.'

Bernadette's face was transformed by a smile. 'Really? You'd do that? You are a true friend to Eddie, so y'are.'

Jed nodded. 'Well, it's the least I can do. Now you get yourself organised, be with Siobhan and come back afterwards. I'll make sure someone calls in on Eddie every day, I promise.' In fact, he knew someone who would be perfect for the role of coordinator and could certainly use the distraction. Penny Morris.

'I can't thank you enough.' As Bernadette went on to explain about her daughter's tricky pregnancy, the visits to hospital and regular bleeding which made them all anxious that poor Siobhan would be able to carry the baby full term, the pile of cards had fanned out onto the bed. One had opened up, and it was then that he saw the message written in black spikey writing. His heart stilled when he read it.

Never forget twelve in the sixth.

He stared at it for an age. He knew with absolute certainty that whoever wrote the card was behind the scam and Eddie's accident. The message was a clear warning to Eddie to not go blabbing to the police. So, all he had to do now was find out who had sent it. Looking at the number of cards Eddie had received this was going to be easier said than done. At least the writing was quite distinctive which might help, though it could be heavily disguised.

'Who sent this card?' Jed managed to modulate his voice to be as casual as he could make it. Bernadette looked at him blankly.

'I haven't a clue. Now I'd better be sorting out me trains, hadn't I?' Her face was a mixture of excitement over the baby and worry about Eddie. As Bernadette went on to explain about her family and other grandchildren, Jed managed to pocket the card, his mind racing. Who had sent the damned thing, because if he could find out then he would definitely discover who was behind the scam. Perhaps, it was Gary? He decided to drive by his house and see if he could find some clue as to where he had gone.

A while later he drew up outside Gary's address and went through his cover story in his mind. The house was a small mid terrace set in the village of Walton down a little narrow street just off the High Street called Knight Lane. Gary lived at number 15. Jed was well aware that he might become a suspect if anything had happened to Gary, so he parked up in the local pub, a sleepy, welcoming looking place and walked the short distance to Gary's house and rapped his knuckle on the front door. All the windows were closed, and the house looked neat, tidy and empty. He walked down the side of the end cottage and found a rear pathway to the back gardens until he found the rear entrance to Gary's house. There was a high fence around the garden and a narrow gate. He reached up and fiddled with the bolt and made his way quietly into Gary's back garden. The rear was mainly laid to lawn with a patio set with a gaily coloured purple parasol still left out from summer. It fluttered forlornly in the wind. He wondered briefly who Gary entertained at his house? He did not strike Jed as a sociable man and was viewed as a morose character, something of an outsider by the other lads. Still, he realised he knew barely anything about the real Gary McKay. The rear of the property had patio doors which led to the kitchen diner. The kitchen looked tidy and the dining room pretty bare, apart from a small pine table and four chairs, a small sideboard and a large racing watercolour of what looked like Desert Orchid, soaring over the last fence at Cheltenham.

He searched around under the various plant pots wondering if Gary kept a spare key anywhere obvious. No such luck. He moved to peer into the kitchen window which again pretty was bare. There were some high stools under the surfaces and a landline phone with a notepad and pen next to it, a few mugs and pans and what looked like a pile of Timeform books and Racing Posts in a heap on the side of the work surface. On one wall, there was a corkboard with a calendar pinned up and a couple of postcards featuring windswept seascapes. One of them had some writing on it. He screwed up his eyes to read it as it may be important. It looked like UIST. Surely that couldn't be right, could it? Dimly he remembered something about the Isle of Uist. Where was it again? He was still pondering this when he heard the gate creak open behind him.

'Can I help you with anything?'

He turned to find himself face to face with an elderly grey haired lady wearing jeans and a large puffa jacket. Her grey hair was swept off her face with an Alice band and her eyes were bright blue and rather suspicious. He smiled warmly.

'Oh, I hope so. I'm just after Gary but he doesn't appear to be in. I needed a quick word.'

He could see her taking in his build and expensive clothes and hesitate.

Jed smiled. 'I'm a jockey like Gary and I wanted to catch up with him about some horses, that's all.'

Jed fished in his pocket for his BHA ID, the one he had forgotten to get changed which read *The Honourable Jedidiah Cavendish,* a title he did not want to use precisely because it always had an effect on people and made them think he was one of the landed gentry which he supposed he was really. He disliked the barrier it created, however. People almost immediately became subservient, pulling their forelocks, or sometimes belligerent. On this occasion, however, it was very useful. The woman looked impressed and relaxed immediately.

'Oh, I see. Well, Mr Cavendish. I'm Gary's landlady, Mrs Kidd.' She stuck out her hand which he shook. 'Gary told me he was going away to see his sister for a few days. '

'Any idea when he'll be back or where the sister lives?'

Mrs Kidd thought for a moment. 'I seem to think somewhere in Scotland, but I can't just recall where.' She smiled, and Jed realised that in her youth she must have been a very attractive woman.

Jed nodded. 'Fine. I'll give him a ring then. Best be on my way.' He suddenly remembered where he knew the name from. Uist, one of the small islands in the Outer Hebrides.

'Thank you, Mrs Kidd, you've been very helpful.'

Gary McKay had decided to up and leave mid season, but now he had a good idea where he may have gone. He had also revised his opinion of Gary's role in the scam. Disappearing to deepest, darkest Scotland smacked of running away and was not the action of a criminal mastermind. Was Gary afraid of suffering the same fate as Eddie? He would check out the four races he was suspicious about and see who had ridden the winners, but he was willing to bet that he knew the answer. When Eddie had won riding Happy Days, number twelve in the sixth race, someone would have lost a lot of money and that had made them very angry indeed, enough to harm Eddie in a fake car accident but also scare off Gary. He wondered if he had seen the same 'Get Well' card he had in his pocket, with its cryptic note, *Never forget twelve in the sixth,* and drawn his own conclusions as to who was behind Eddie's so called 'accident'?

Chapter 18

Marcus looked truly awful. He had a black eye, several other cuts and bruises and a couple of fractured ribs. His face was pasty under the purpling bruises, and he looked ten years older. Imogen wondered what had happened to the charming youth who had whistled and joked around and never had a care in the world. A wave of sadness washed over her. She was sure that the same old Marcus was in there somewhere beneath this macho, tight lipped exterior. Underneath, she knew he was scared and that was why he was keeping his own counsel about what had happened.

'Nah, it was nothing, just a misunderstanding that was all.'

Imogen and her mother had been granted a special visit to see him following the assault. In the small room in the presence of one prison officer and just the three of them, they hoped he would tell them what had happened and who was behind the assault.

Mrs James had sobbed when she had first seen her son and now this gave way to anger.

'But what are the authorities supposed to do if you don't tell them who hit you? It's madness, Marcus. And you're supposed to be getting out soon.'

'Mum is right. Come on Marcus. Just tell the authorities who is involved, and they'll be able to help you.'

Marcus shook his head and sneered. 'Look, it's not the way things work around here.' He glanced at the prison officer who at least had the decency to look away and give them some privacy. 'If I say something then things will only get worse. I'll just keep my head down and I'll be out of here in a couple of months.' He flexed his fingers, his jaw tense. He attempted a smile. 'Don't worry. This looks worse than it is. It'll heal in no time.'

Imogen knew there was a code of silence amongst criminals and suspected what Marcus was saying was probably true. Mrs James's face crumpled.

'Just tell us Marcus. We can talk to a solicitor, get you moved, anything…'

Marcus shook his head. 'I'm glad you came but believe me I know what I'm doing. I'll be out and gone in no time, but for now I've just got to get through this.'

Imogen decided to change the subject and Marcus gave her a grateful look as Mrs James relaxed slightly and began to talk about what was going on in the community. As they were leaving Imogen hugged her brother taking great care not to squeeze his ribcage. She took the opportunity to whisper in his ear.

'Was it to do with the betting system you mentioned?'

A look of deep shock and fear flashed over Marcus's face. He quickly recovered himself.

'What are you on about, sis?' he hissed.

But in the age old way that big sisters know pretty much everything about their siblings, Imogen knew from the expression he tried so hard to hide, that she had hit the nail on the head. Perhaps, someone had overheard them discussing it in the visitors' room, heard Marcus boasting about his betting prowess. She cast her mind back to the visiting room and who else was there and could have overheard Eddie going on about betting and heard her ask him about Eddie O'Neill, because someone in that room was involved in the scam, she was sure of it. She also knew that she couldn't ask for any more details, because to do so would place Marcus in even greater danger. Her mother's tear stained face was a real spur to sort through the research she had undertaken to try and find some answers. She was meeting Jed later and was desperate to have something concrete for him. Marcus, Eddie, her family and Jed, were all depending on her.

Back in her room she painstakingly went through the four horses that Jed thought were definitely prevented from winning by his analysis of Eddie's riding. She transferred her scribbles onto a large sheet of paper, the horse's name in the middle with various other facts about the horse, its owners, trainers, jockeys and racecourses where they had lost, every single conceivable fact she could find, even the colour of the horse and gender. Surprisingly, there was so much data available on the internet it was relatively easy to amass a huge amount of information on each race. Then she did the same for the next horse, painstakingly cross checking the information as she went. Ignoring her thirst and grumbling stomach, she persisted and laid the paper out in front of her, scanning the results of her labour. She glanced at her watch and realised she was late, so she bundled the papers into her bag, grabbed her coat and went to meet Jed.

Jed was waiting at the restaurant, sipping a glass of sparkling water when she came in. As usual he kissed her on both cheeks, and she flushed a little less this time. She felt she should have been getting used to his continental greeting by now, but each time he took her by surprise. She smelt some expensive spicy cologne and felt his strong muscles ripple as he dipped his head to kiss her. For a brief moment, she wondered what it would be like to run her fingers through his dark curls and then berated herself. They had serious things to discuss. They had ordered their food, a light salad for Jed and salmon en croute for Imogen and settled down to discuss their findings. Jed explained about Bernadette and the promise he had made about visiting Eddie.

'I've asked Penny Morris to make up a rota with the lads so that Eddie has regular visits, but there are still a few spaces left if you can manage anything. You might be able to suss out who else visits?'

'OK.' Imogen was a little uncertain. She had never met Eddie before and certainly had no experience of visiting anyone in a coma. It would feel odd, almost voyeuristic to visit a stranger. Still, she could see the merit in Jed's ideas. 'I can probably manage the odd visit. Did you find out anything else? How was Hugh Mitchell's place?'

Jed speared a forkful of green leaves. 'A bit strange. Hugh Mitchell is either a reclusive or hardly ever there. The yard seems to be run by the Assistant trainer, a Frenchman called Anton Du Pre. But there was something else…' Jed shook his head, 'it might be nothing but there was a shipping container there that had a whole load of heavy duty ironmongery on it. It just made me wonder what might be in there. I wonder if he is using drugs to enhance his horses' performances and perhaps that is where the stuff is stored. And another jockey, Gary MacKay, has disappeared and, I think it may be to do with this card.'

He fished in his pocket for the 'Get well' card with its cryptic message,

Never forget twelve in the sixth.

The hairs on Imogen's neck stood up as she read it, turning the card over and over to inspect it. After a while, she spoke.

'Well, that's interesting because Gary McKay is the jockey who rides the winners for Hugh Mitchell in the races where Eddie pulled his horses. I didn't realise it at first because a different jockey was listed to ride, but then Gary stepped up at the last minute.'

Imogen looked round the restaurant which was virtually empty. Still, the experience with Marcus made her feel slightly on edge. She pulled out the pieces of paper from her bag and spread them on the table.

'I have tried to be systematic about this and looked at a range of variables for each of Eddie's rides, you were worried about. I haven't really had time to look at it yet.' Imogen didn't know whether to mention Marcus and what had happened or not.

Jed whistled and studied each piece of paper carefully. He turned the paper this way and that.

Finally, he spoke. 'Interesting.'

'What?'

'Look.' He pointed at the paper. 'All the horses that won when Eddie's didn't are owned by syndicates, Sport of Kings Racing and Winning Streak Group.'

He pointed at the relevant section for each horse.

He was right. Imogen had studied the losing horses in the main and had only added the winners as an afterthought. Then again was it significant?

'Are syndicates common in racing?'

'Increasingly yes. It allows people to enjoy racing yet share the costs and the risk across a number of parties. The skill is in managing payments, communication and so on across a group, but the beauty is that you don't even need stables because the horses are in training. All you need is an office somewhere. But it might not be relevant.'

Imogen made some more notes. 'So, in terms of connections all the horses were favourites, ridden by Eddie, are owned by syndicates, ran in northern courses where Richard Kendrick was the steward and the eventual winners were all from Hugh Mitchell's yard. They were all ridden by Gary MacKay, at the last minute, who has since gone missing.' She frowned. 'Hmm. Look, I also included the prize money of the race and distance. And we know about the steward, Richard Kendrick, officiating at each of the race meetings.'

Jed noticed that the prize money varied, and the races were well over two miles, nearer three, which was on the longer side for national hunt racing. Was that relevant? He had no idea. He tried to pull all the information together to see if he could make any more links. Imogen tried to so the same.

'So, it can't be a coincidence that Gary McKay rode the winners that Eddie pulled, but why would he be in on it? Surely if you pull a race then the next best horse wins, so if you bet on the next best horse then why do you also need another accomplice?'

Jed studied her. 'Well, I suppose it's about ensuring that the horse you have doped actually wins. The jockey, in this case Gary Mackay, is tipped the wink, and pushes his horse to win, by hook or by crook. He has a reputation for rough riding, so he'd be perfect. Knowing the favourite is being pulled would be a huge advantage in positioning, racing strategy and so on.'

Imogen took this in. She tended to think in logical, straight lines, but she was forgetting that horses were animals and therefore not entirely predictable and then ridden by humans who were fallible too.

'Do you think Gary has disappeared of his own accord? Might he have been kidnapped to silence him, or perhaps he is the brains behind the operation?'

Jed went on the explain about his visit to Gary's house and his theory about him disappearing to the Isle of Uist.

Jed summarised their findings. 'So, we believe Eddie was blackmailed and we think it was to do with the affair he was having with Geraldine McLoughlin. There could be links to the criminal fraternity and the horses that won when horses were pulled were trained by Hugh Mitchell and ridden by Gary Mackay. And Hugh Mitchell has a shipping container with some very heavy duty ironmongery on it to protect it.'

Jed picked up the card again. 'So, all we need to do is find out who has written this to find out who is behind the attack. At least if we're visiting Eddie then we can keep an eye on who is coming and going, I suppose. The criminals might pop in to keep an eye on things.'

Imogen considered this. She turned over one of the pieces of paper and started to write.

'So, you need to investigate Hugh Mitchell's shipping container, ask everyone who visits Eddie who the other visitors are. What else?' She sighed half wondering whether to say anything about Marcus. Was she overreacting? It had all seemed to clear in the prison but outside it she was less sure. Had she imagined his reaction?

Jed caught her hesitation. 'Are you alright? You seem a bit preoccupied.'

Imogen nodded. 'Yes and no. There's been some problems with Marcus, that's all. He was beaten up in prison and he won't really say anything about who did it or why.' She paused. 'I asked him if it was anything to do with the betting system he spoke about, but he denied it. I just get the feeling that one of the other prisoners has overheard him boasting about the system to us when he was supposed to keep his mouth shut and maybe it's payback for that.'

Jed looked thoughtful. 'I suppose there are lots of other prisoners around and their visitors when you visit. Have you noticed anyone looking or listening?'

'Yes. We are usually sitting next to the same middle aged guy whose two sons visit him, at least I think they are his sons. Sometimes, I think they've been listening into our conversations. One of the boys was leaning right back on his chair and could have heard Marcus.'

Jed shrugged. 'But prisoners fighting from time to time is not really unusual, is it? It might be to do with something entirely unrelated, especially if your brother is a bit on the mouthy side. They could have argued about anything.'

Imogen winced at Jed's description of Marcus, but it was true. She did feel a little but put out that Jed wasn't taking her seriously. Maybe it was her? Imogen studied the lists.

'So, what do we do next?'

There was silence as they both tried to search for something tangible to grasp. It was rather like trying to find the end of a ball of wool that was very well hidden.

'Well, we could start by a bit of breaking and entering...'

Imogen gasped. 'Do you know what to do? I didn't have you down as someone who would be capable of such a thing. You're far too posh.'

Jed grinned. 'I did have some dubious mates back in the day, so I reckon I can give it a go. Besides, I'm desperate to know what's in Hugh Mitchell's shipping container. It must be valuable or something he doesn't want anyone else to know about. I'll ring you when I'm done.' He grinned. 'Mind you, I will have to be careful. I wouldn't want to offend my future employers, now would I?'

'Future employers?'

'Yes. I'm taking Gary McKay's rides at Hugh Mitchell's place, mind you, I can't just rock up and start breaking into the storage container in broad daylight. I'll just have to suss it out, find out the routines, see when the place is quiet...'

Imogen bristled. 'There's no way you get to have all the fun. Surely, you'll need someone to hold the torch or something. I'm definitely coming with you.'

Jed laughed. 'OK. You're on.'

Jed was up with the lark and went for a jog the next morning. When he arrived back home DI Roberts was waiting for him with his companion DC Cooper. He guessed they had progressed their investigations or maybe it was about Gary?

'Now then Sir. Might we just have a quick word.' DI Roberts smiled, but the smile didn't quite reach his eyes.

Jed showed them in and offered them a cup of tea which they readily accepted.

'I only have Earl Grey, if that's alright.' Jed ignored DC Cooper's grimace. 'So, what can help you with?'

DI Roberts took a sip of tea, whilst his companion sniffed at it suspiciously.

'We just need to catch up with you, that's all.'

'Have you found anything out?'

DI Roberts paused. 'Well, as we said before we are following several different lines of inquiry, but there's nothing conclusive at present. When we met last time, you said mentioned a phone call that Mr O'Neill took before his race. The one you picked up. We just wondered what you thought *twelve in the sixth* might mean?'

Jed shrugged. It seemed that maybe the police had had their dehydration theory blown away after all.

'It could mean anything. I did wonder if it might be connected to the race he was about to ride in…'

'In which he was riding a horse number twelve, I believe, the favourite which he won on…'

'Yes, that's right.'

DC Cooper placed his untouched cup on the table.

'Did it occur to you that the phone call might be a message or instruction to pull the race?'

There was a silence as they both peered at him. 'Well, it could have meant that, it could also have meant anything… Anyway, I forgot to pass the message on.'

DI Roberts pursed his lips. 'And Mr O'Neill won on the favourite. I presume racing is well regulated and you have rules about jockeys not trying or deliberately holding up their horse, so if anyone had any concerns about Eddie O'Neill's riding it wouldn't have gone unnoticed.'

'God, yes. We can't do anything without the stewards scrutinising the race on monitors. If there was anything dodgy then the stewards would have been onto it like a flash.'

'Quite so, quite so,' replied DI Roberts.

'And you were you aware of a steward's inquiry in that race?' asked DC Cooper.

'No, there wasn't one. There was no reason to have one.'

'So, I presume there are several stewards who we could speak to about Mr O'Neill's riding to see if there were any concerns?'

'Yes. Stewards are volunteers except for stipendiary stewards who are paid by the BHA and advise the others. There is usually one at each meeting, sometimes more.'

DI Roberts brightened. 'Really? Does the stipendiary steward cover a particular area?'

'Yes, but they can be asked to go anywhere.'

'Who is the steward at Uttoxeter racecourse?'

It was someone that Jed knew by sight but hadn't met before. Someone who had featured in his and Imogen's discussions.

'Someone called Richard Kendrick, I believe. You should be able to contact him via the BHA.'

Both men stirred.

DI Roberts smiled fully this time. 'Thank you, Mr Cavendish, you have been very helpful.'

As they were leaving, DI Roberts added. 'You wouldn't happen to have heard of a jockey called Gary MacKay, would you?'

'Yes. I know him. Last I heard he hadn't turned up to ride out and appears to have disappeared.' He wondered how much to reveal and decided to be completely open and honest. 'As a matter of fact, I went to see Gary. I'd been offered some rides of his and wanted to check them out with him.'

DI Roberts nodded. 'But you didn't find him, I presume?'

'No, that's right. His landlady said he'd gone to stay with his sister in Scotland, I believe.'

DS Cooper piped up. 'Any idea whereabouts in Scotland?'

Jed shook his head. 'No, I'm afraid I don't.' He had no intention of doing all the work for them. 'Do you think he's OK, just upping and leaving mid season is quite a strange thing to do, after all?'

The two police officers looked at each other.

'Quite but then people disappear all the time, Sir. We see it a lot on our line of work, don't we Sergeant?' DS Cooper nodded sagely.

As they left Jed wondered if he had underestimated them and what their inquiries would reveal.

Chapter 19

Jed had been wanting to meet Richard Kendrick, but not necessarily in the circumstances he found himself in. It was a cool but bright day at Wetherby and he had several runners; a couple for Kieron McLoughlin and one for Lydia Fox and another for Hugh Mitchell. It was in the first when he was riding the second favourite Bad Karma that the problems started. The chestnut gelding started off well and Jed felt the familiar thrill of the wind in his face until the horse got too close to the second to last fence and banged his pastern. Jed thought they'd got away with it, until the gelding sprang over the last fence. He was positioned in second place behind Charlie Durrant's ride and was just about to make his run four hundred yards or so from home, when he felt the horse tire as though he had run out of fuel. He was also rolling about all over the place, as though he was in pain. Jed gave the horse a couple of light smacks with his whip, just to make sure, but this had only a very small effect. The horse rallied for a few strides before decelerating further. Jed tried to push on with his

heels and hands as he saw Charlie Durrant's green colours disappear into the distance and other horses begin to overtake. Damn. Today definitely wasn't going to be their day. The horse felt slightly uneven. The knock must have begun to hurt by now. Jed decided not to push any further as he knew from experience that he wouldn't catch the leaders, so he slowed down and finished the race at comfortable canter coming in just out of the placings in sixth.

Kieron was waiting for him looking worried.

'What happened there? I thought we were in with a shout.'

Jed had dismounted and watched as Kieron ran his fingers over the horse's legs. Jed waited for him to reappear from under the horse's belly.

'There's no injury and he doesn't look lame. So, what happened?'

Jed shrugged. 'He had a knock second from home. It didn't feel too bad. Then it was as though he had reached a wall and he just felt not lame exactly, but uneven as though something was hurting. So, I decided not to push him to get a place. I didn't want to make things worse.'

Kieron nodded. 'OK. I'll have the lads hose his legs for a bit to stop any swelling coming out.' He asked the stable girl to take him back to the stable. 'No worries, Jed.' He gave him a curt nod before he dashed off under the railings to talk to the worried owners. Jed was just relieved that Kieron was such a good horseman that he also had no desire to push the horse beyond his limits risking injury and staleness.

However, that wasn't the end of the matter. Just as he was changing for the next race, he was surprised to be asked by the valet to step inside the steward's office.

There were two stewards he knew by sight, Stephen Todd and Michael Mountford. The third man he didn't know, but he was soon introduced as none other than Richard Kendrick. Kieron McLoughlin was also present and nodded as Jed strode in.

The men were watching a replay of the first race on three monitors at the point where Bad Karma had started to falter, and Jed had given him a couple of cracks with his whip.

Richard Kendrick was younger than he expected, tall and slim in a grey suit, he had the palest blue eyes Jed had ever seen. His manner was brisk and rather patronising.

'Now then Mr Cavendish. We would like a word about your mount's poor performance in the first race. He was well fancied, and he should have been placed at least. What happened?'

Jed went on to explain. 'Well Sir, I'm not sure. He tired as though he had hit a brick wall and he felt a little uneven, not lame exactly. I gave him a couple of cracks with the whip to see if he had anything left. He rallied briefly and then fell back again.'

The men looked at each other as Kendrick replayed the DVD. They stopped the clip just after he had whipped the horse. An attractive brunette was making notes and looked sympathetically at him. Jed felt his palms start to sweat. He felt at a considerable disadvantage dressed in his undershirt and breeches, whereas his accusers were wearing suits and shiny shoes. He'd been before the stewards before, but it was usually over something much more obvious like an obstruction and on those occasions, he had been the injured party, riding the horse hampered by the conduct of another jockey.

'So, Mr McLoughlin. Could I ask how the horse is now? If what the jockey says is correct, then I would expect some lameness or some sort of injury. Did you find anything like that when you checked him?'

Kieron looked uncomfortable. 'Not as such, Sir. I had the lads hosing his legs down, yer know, hoping the cold water will sort it out. He must have had a knock as he's jumped over a hurdle, that's all.'

Kendrick contorted his features into an unpleasant sneer.

'Well, we have checked the footage and at no time can we see any such incident.'

Jed felt fury rise through him like a volcano, but he bit his lip. How on earth would these idiots who had no doubt been watching the race from the comfort of the stands or the bar have any idea what had happened during the race?

With considerable self control he took a deep breath. 'The horse did get very close to the second last and knocked his pastern. There was no injury or abrasion, but it was enough of a knock to hurt him and ruin his chances.'

Richard Kendrick surveyed him coldly, his pale eyes boring into him as he played with his Mont Blanc pen.

'Well, we'll just have to take your word for it, otherwise you could face a disciplinary hearing for not trying.' He glanced at his colleagues, but it was clear that they were in awe of him. One of the other men cleared his throat and appeared about to speak, but Kendrick silenced him with a glance. Jed took the opportunity to make a point.

'Well Sir, I didn't think it was in the horse's interests to risk greater injury by pushing him further. I do have to take into account the welfare of the animal, as all jockeys do.''

'That's true Sir. I have complete faith in Mr Cavendish,' Kieron continued.

Kendrick paced up and down before turning to face them. 'So, it's your first season as a professional jockey, I take it?'

'Yes, that's right, sir.' He gave Jed a further penetrating stare as he played with the thick wedding ring on his left finger of his left hand. Jed remembered that Tristan had said he had a very rich wife. His hands were slim and pale and his fingers long. One of the other stewards coughed awkwardly. Still, Richard Kendrick stared at him. Jed had the feeling he was enjoying making them wait to hear his verdict. Eventually he appeared to come to a decision.

'Well, let's hope we don't see you in here again, Cavendish. Consider yourself warned, we could just as easily have suspended you for not trying. Remember that we have the integrity of the sport in our hands. Now, you may leave.' He flapped his fingers at them as though swatting away an annoying fly.

Both Jed and Kieron muttered their thanks and left. Jed noticed Kendrick watching him yet again and had the feeling he had made an enemy.

'Is he always like that?' Jed asked. Kieron shook his head.

'Not at all.' He shrugged. 'He is usually pretty reasonable, I'd say. Probably having a bad day.'

They said their goodbyes and Kieron asked him to take some more of his rides. At least Kieron wasn't making an issue of his riding. As Jed made his way home another disquieting thought occurred to him. If Kendrick was usually quite reasonable, why had he picked him up over such a small point as not pushing an injured horse? He had the distinct feeling that he was being warned off. No doubt he had realised after the police had visited, that it was Jed that had given them his name. Still, it wasn't as though they wouldn't have thought of it themselves. He had the strangest feeling that Kendrick was merely flexing his muscles, showing Jed his strength. He wondered why the police visit had rattled him. Was he just simply angry, or did he have something to hide?

When he arrived home, he was surprised to see Arabella's sporty Audi parked outside his house. Damn, that was all he needed. They had knocked around for a couple of years, but then Arabella had become a little more serious and clingy. Jed had found the more she clung the more he had fled in the opposite direction, so much so, they had split up. Then recently she had changed her tactics and taken to popping up at unexpected moments with studied casualness, as though she was reminding him of what he was missing. She said she simply wanted to remain friends, but Jed was not at all convinced. As soon as she saw him arrive, she leapt out of her car.

'Darling, I was passing and since you haven't returned my calls about the party, I popped into remind you.' Arabella rose to her feet and planted a kiss on Jed's lips. Her blonde hair was held back by a fur headband and she was swathed in a huge coat. It felt churlish for Jed to turn his face away from her, but for a second, he found himself considering it.

Arabella flicked her hair and eyed him slyly.

'What are you really doing here, Arabella?'

She pouted. 'Well, you haven't answered my calls or returned my messages so what's a girl to do? Have you forgotten about Henry's party?'

Henry was Arabella's banker brother who was holding his birthday party at Mulberry House. Jed had forgotten, the invite was somewhere on his mantlepiece. Clearly, Arabella still expected him to escort her.

'I had forgotten, I'm busy riding these days trying to make a name for myself, I'm pretty exhausted…'

Arabella pouted and stood on her tiptoes, her eyes imploring. 'Please. Henry would be so thrilled, and that Felicity Hill is going to be there and one of her jockey friends, Jake someone or other, so you can always talk horses…'

Jed looked into Arabella's soulless blue eyes and reconsidered. Henry was an old friend, he could probably keep Arabella at arms' length, but the opportunity to study Felicity and Jake close up was very tempting. Keep an open mind and explore all lines of inquiry, Imogen had said, and this opportunity had just dropped into his lap.

'OK. I'll pick you up for nine.'

Arabella tried, but failed to hide her delight.

Jed had planned to appear to drink whilst substituting his wine for sparkling water, so that he was now watching very drunk people making absolute fools of themselves. This, he reflected, was quite a sobering experience in itself. The birthday bash was held at Arabella and Henry's parents' home, Mulberry House. There was a fabulous buffet of smoked salmon, beef and pork complete with delicious salads, chocolate fountains with bowls full of strawberries and a magnificent birthday cake shaped into a rugby pitch. Henry was far more into rugby than racing, he recalled. The alcohol flowed freely with hundreds of bottles of champagne, spirits and cocktails being consumed. Waiters in black and white circulated continuously. Arabella was dancing rather wildly having quaffed several glasses of champagne and was at the stage where she loved everything and everyone.

Jed was attempting to chat to Jake Horton who had also knocked back several glasses and had his arm possessively draped around Felicity Hill. Felicity's choice of outfit was even more provocative than her race day attire. She wore a virtually see through, figure hugging white dress with a plunge neckline adorned with pink roses, skyscraper pink heels and killer pink nails. Her hair was twisted up and held in place by clips with rose fastenings. As usual her skin was an extraordinary orange colour.

'It's great to see you,' Jed shouted to Jake over the music. 'How do you know Henry?'

Jake shrugged. 'Some friends of Felicity invited us...' He seemed rather wired and watchful. Felicity smiled and was side-tracked by a friend who she greeted with enormous and rather fake air kisses. A pair of girls whose clothes left little to the imagination, gossiped and giggled, scanning the crowd. They spoke to a passing waiter and pointed out Jake. The waiter approached and whispered in Jake's ear. Jake grinned and smiled at the two girls.

'Just need to sign some autographs for some fans,' he muttered with a wink as he strode off towards the fans, before leaving the room with them. Jed strained to see what was going on and slipped out after them. They disappeared into a side room which had several men huddled outside. Jed didn't recognise any of them, but their demeanour was wary as he approached.

Jed made to go into the room but was blocked by one of the burlier men.

'Hey, what's going on here,' Jed deliberately slurred his words. 'Why can't I go in? I'm just following me mate, that's all.'

'Never you mind,' muttered the dark haired, thick set man, who had the look of a bouncer. 'Looks like you've had enough of the old vino, never mind anything else. Be a good chap and turn right round.'

Jed did so with a shrug but having the advantage of knowing the layout of the house, he wandered down another corridor and found the entrance to the same room was blocked by a few heavies too. Jed was certain that Jake and the girls had gone into the room and he wondered what the hell was going on in there. He waited for about an hour when he heard doors opening. He walked back down the corridor as he heard the two girls, the fans, approaching, chatting to each other. Jed hid behind the curtains on the hallway window. Thankfully they were full length curtains, so he was completely obscured.

'Easiest money I've ever earned. We didn't have to do nuffin', just drape ourselves round that guy and wait for them to take the pics. It was a piece of cake, Chan.'

'You sure that was it? I don't want no trouble. What do they want the pics for?'

'I dunno but it's nothing to do wi' us as long as we get paid, is it?'

'Who's taking us back?'

'The blonde guy, you know, Daz.'

Jed waited for the girls to pass and slid out of the window. Jed loitered outside to see where the girls went. It was cold and damp. He waited in the gloom, when his patience was rewarded as about half an hour later, he saw the two girls getting into a silver saloon driven by a short blond man. He followed in his Mercedes at a distance. As the car drove under a streetlamp, Jed tried to see who was driving. He briefly saw the lean face of a man before the lights dappled into darkness. The girls were dropped at the end of a residential street and made their way into a large house. He made a note of the property number and name, The Limes. Jed turned around to drive back to the party to check on Arabella, his head reeling. He had Jake down as a straightforward sort of a lad, but he had to wonder what had just happened. Surely it didn't take an hour to simply sign some autographs? Another thought nagged away at him. The blond man who had driven the girls looked vaguely familiar, but for the life of him he couldn't think where he had seen him before.

Chapter 20

Imogen sat in the hospital room peering at the still figure of Eddie O Neill. She felt sadness, embarrassment and a sense of voyeurism. He looked so peaceful, as though he was asleep. Yet here she was an interloper intruding on him when she was simply a complete stranger. He had a large bandage around his head and his face was mottled with healing cuts and bruises. Jed had contacted Penny Morris and she had managed to draw up a rota of visitors and today it was her turn.

Eddie was attached by leads and tubes to various monitors. There was a row of 'Get Well' cards and several vases of flowers placed at in the corner of the room. Imogen had read how it was vitally important to try to communicate with someone in a coma. Something, however small, might just trigger a reaction and bring the person back to the land of the living. She held Eddie's limp hand and began to speak in a low voice.

'Hi there, Eddie. I'm Imogen, a friend of Jed's. We've never met before, but I've heard a lot about you. It's a lovely day. I think Jed is racing today and your mother had had to go back to Ireland, so she asked me to pop in. Your sister is having a baby. She will be back as soon as she can. We all want you get better and we know you can do it. Would you like me to read the racing results?' She picked up the paper and started to read out yesterday's results. Twenty minutes must have passed, and she had got over the initial embarrassment of hearing herself speak to a total stranger who probably could not even hear her. However, the enormity of the situation, seeing Eddie in the flesh, made her press on. She was convinced that all that needed was the neurones

169

to start making connections and then he could start to recover. She decided to speak about the accident and about their suspicions.

'Look. We don't know exactly what happened, but we've a pretty good idea. We know about the betting scam and you being paid to pull races and we're trying to find out who is behind it. We don't blame you, we think that you were being blackmailed and maybe had to do it. Jed and I are trying to find out what happened. We're making some headway and we really will do all we can to help you.' Was it her imagination or did Eddie's hand start to feel slightly warmer? She put it down to the combination of their combined body heat. Her throat was dry from all the talking so she decided to get a coffee, giving Eddie's hand an extra squeeze before she left.

As she fished in her bag for some change for the machine, she wracked her brains trying to think of how to help Eddie. There was well documented research about the merits of talking to coma patients, playing them their favourite music and using familiar people and voices. She made a mental note to ask Jed what music Eddie liked, there was bound to be lots of it in his home and she could have a word with the nurses about playing the stuff. The dreadfulness of his situation really hit home to her. Seeing him in the bed, fragile and vulnerable was a real reminder that his life hung in the balance and she and Jed had to help him. No-one else knew the full story, the police seemed to be happy to believe that the accident was due to dehydration, so it was down to her and Jed. They were the only ones who could do anything. She felt this burden weighing heavily upon her.

As she made her way back past the nurses' station, she saw that the Eddie has another visitor, a slender, fragile looking woman in her thirties. She had long dark hair and her eyes were full of tears. Imogen hovered outside the room, not wanting to intrude on the woman's grief as she sat opposite the door. She was speaking to Eddie in a low urgent voice. Imogen recognised her immediately from the photo. Geraldine. Even in a distressed state she was still a very attractive woman.

'Come on Eddie. You must get better, darling, I don't know what I'd do without you. Remember our plans? We can still do it, Eddie. All you have to do is come back to me, my darling. Come back to me…'

Imogen cleared her throat and stepped into view. The woman gasped and stood up as if to leave.

'Please don't leave on my account. You see, Eddie is in trouble and I think you can help. I'm Imogen, a friend of Jed's. I recognise you from your photo, Geraldine. We really need to talk.'

Geraldine dabbed her eyes and composed herself.

'It's just he is such a lovely person. Kieron and I just love having him as our stable jockey. He has a kind word for everyone, it was just so hard seeing him there.'

Imogen sipped her coffee and wondered how she could broach the topic of their affair. She couldn't admit to overhearing what Geraldine had said to Eddie and of course, Geraldine wasn't going to tell her about her relationship just like that. After all, she didn't know Imogen and was hardly likely to start confessing to her about her private life. Not for the first time, Imogen really wished that Jed was there to help her. He could talk to Geraldine as a friend. As Eddie's best mate, he was in quite a different situation. She decided to go for the direct approach.

'It's really hard when you are as close as you two.' She brushed away Geraldine's momentary shock. 'Look. I know you don't know me, but I am a friend of Jed's.' The woman opened her mouth as though to protest, but Imogen ploughed on.

'Jed consulted me when the police told him that they believed Eddie had probably just blacked out as a result of being dehydrated. I am a research assistant into the effects of drugs and I would say from the blood tests, it was unlikely given the timing of the incident. It happened after the race, when Eddie had made the weights he would have been thirsty and drank to alleviate this, after all he wasn't racing again for another three days.'

All sorts of emotions flickered over Geraldine's face as she took this in.

'So, what you're saying is that Eddie's car accident was caused deliberately? But why?'

Imogen took a sip of her drink. 'As you know Jed is Eddie's best friend and he really wants to help Eddie. We think Eddie may have been blackmailed into stopping horses…'

Geraldine gasped and began to get up.

'I won't sit here and listen to all these lies…'

'Listen to me. Eddie's life might well be in danger if you don't. Whatever you say will be treated in the strictest of confidence, we know about you and Eddie but someone else did too. Whoever, that person is, may well have tried to kill Eddie and we have to catch them…'

Geraldine glowered at her.

'Whatever you think you know, you're wrong.'

Imogen nodded. 'Why don't you sit down and fill me in on the details or speak to Jed. You know him, at least.' She tried to reassure the woman. 'Look, I know how hard this must be for you…'

Geraldine gave a look full of contempt. 'You have absolutely no idea. And I will speak to Jed and find out what the hell is going on.' With that she turned on her heel and left, but Imogen knew she was rattled, and she expected her to ring Jed sooner rather than later. She was kicking herself though for pushing too hard. She was after all a stranger to Geraldine. However, Geraldine's one-way conversation with Eddie certainly confirmed to her that they were on the right lines.

They drove to Hugh Mitchell's place, Jed in his swish, black Mercedes. It occurred to Imogen that it was a very expensive car for a young jockey just starting out in the profession. Jed seemed to be a man of private means. She realised that there was a lot she didn't know about Jed. The cultured tones and references to private education, hinted at a monied background. Yet there was a realness about him, he never gave too much away, got on with everyone, was socially skilled and respectful of people. She made a mental note to google him or check out his profile in the Racing Post. She felt uneasy with very posh people, but also slightly impressed if she was brutally honest. Yet she hated herself for it. Her own aspiring middle class background resulted in people who just tried too hard. Jed had the sort of self-confidence and nonchalance that didn't care what people thought, the sort of poise that only those born into money possessed.

Jed filled her in on his encounter with Richard Kendrick. Imogen's eyes widened as he spoke.

'So, he had you in for not trying because you didn't push an injured horse?'

'Yeah, that's about the size of it. The horse knocked his pastern, his leg, on the second to last fence, seemed OK for a bit and then he just slowed down. He didn't feel right. There was no point risking further injury by pushing him for a place.'

'If he was so picky about that, how on earth did Eddie get away with pulling races?'

'Exactly. I have been asking questions about Kendrick in the weighing room and put the police onto him, so I suppose he thinks I'm questioning him and he's warning me off.'

Imogen considered this. 'Who have you spoken to?'

'Oh, Lydia, some lads in the weighing room and the police, perhaps the word has got around? Fortunately, Kieron McLoughlin backed me to the hilt, so they didn't have a case.'

Imogen went through her encounter with Geraldine.

'Hmm. I did overhear her talking to Eddie though and I'm pretty sure that they were in a relationship just by what she said.'

'Did she say if she's seen anyone hanging around Eddie? Anyone suspicious?'

Imogen frowned. 'No, she might tell you though. She just stood up and left when I pushed her.'

'Yeah. She has left me a voicemail, so I'll give her a ring.' He went on to tell Imogen about the party.

'So, what do you make of it? I'm pretty sure drugs were being used and that Jake Horton was on something. I'm not sure who the girls were talking about when they mentioned the photos, but it sounded distinctly dodgy.'

'Perhaps, they're just girls having fun?' Imogen thought back to the antics of some of her students which was riotous on occasions.

Jed shrugged. 'Could be. I know where they live, and I might have a word with their parents, as they could turn out to be underage. It's just not right.'

Imogen laughed. 'I think we're getting carried away because none of that explains Eddie's strange phone call and him pulling horses.' Jed began to decelerate and came to halt. Imogen peered out into the inky blackness.

Jed flicked on the internal car light and handed her a dark coat, gloves and a hat. He fished in his pocket and pulled out a set of lock picks.

'There's a torch in the back. Come on let's go.'

'What are we hoping to find again?'

'I have no idea. It just seems suspicious to me. Hugh or Anton are trying to protect something.'

Imogen took a deep breath. She had never been involved in anything remotely criminal before and suddenly it felt wrong. Then she thought back to Eddie lying in the hospital bed, pale and motionless. They had to do this for him, so the ends justified the means.

Several minutes later after she had followed Jed up a narrow pathway past the house and away from the stables where the horses popped their heads over the doors to stare at them, she felt sick with nerves. It had started to drizzle, and her hand was aching as she held the torch and watched Jed insert different sizes of keys into the lock, prodded about a bit, swore and then tried again. Imogen kept shifting her gaze to the house where the downstairs windows to one side twinkled against the dark. Someone was in there. She could hear the horses shuffling and moving about. Imogen clenched her tired muscles and tried to hold the torch steady. She pulled up her hood and shivered. He was taking an age. Still, it was probably good to know that Jed didn't make a habit of picking locks, as he was clearly not an expert. She heard the rustle of some animal in the undergrowth behind them and a dog barking in the distance, as she watched Jed insert different picks and twist them this way and that.

Jed cursed some more before inserting another pick. He twisted the pick and there was a loud click. Finally, the door opened. The torch light picked out his grin.

'Eureka. Come on, let's have a look around.' Jed pulled the door open and they both stepped inside the container.

They padded around, careful to step softly so as not to make too much noise on the metal floor. Imogen swung the light around whilst Jed looked through the contents. To one side there were long coloured poles, wings and fillers.

Jed picked them up. 'Show jumps, excellent quality.'

Imogen swung the torch slowly from the one side to the other. There were layers of white boarding neatly piled in one corner. Jed picked them up. Then there were more poles, large wings, a water tray and yet more poles. To one end there were several large crates. Jed motioned for Imogen to shine the torch nearer and he delved in. He brought out a bottle of red wine. Cote de Nuit.

'Bloody hell. There's loads of them.' Jed pulled out his phone and took a photo of the label. 'It's bloody expensive stuff, worth a bomb, not quite what I was expecting, but still.' They both looked at each other as they heard the sound of cursing and the heavy footfall of someone outside.

'Bloody hell, sod it, bugger…' A voice cursed in a low, slurred tone as they missed their step. 'Bloody Anton, never there when you need 'im, hey?' The voice was getting nearer and nearer. Whoever it was could be seen in the distance, a light bobbing in their hand. He was clearly very drunk. Jed closed the storage container door and whispered to Imogen.

'Looks like he's coming this way. Run like hell as soon as I give the word.'

Imogen realised she was holding her breath as they waited for the man to reach the container. They heard the jangle of metal, as he fished into his pocket for the key.

'Now run!'

Jed pushed the door open with all his might, knocking the inebriated man over in the process. Imogen ran after him, the chilly air filling her lungs, her chest thumping as they ran through the yard and down the lane to where Jed had parked his car. Once inside they roared off in the Mercedes, as its headlights lit up the inky, black sky.

Jed grabbed Imogen's hand as laughter bubbled out of him. Not for the first time, Imogen realised just how much Jed thrived on danger.

'You've got to admit, it's not the best way to meet your future employer, is it?'

'That was Hugh Mitchell?'

'I'd say so and clearly he is a reclusive alcoholic. Still, at least he was so pissed he probably won't remember the incident.'

Imogen laughed too, but mainly from relief.

'Are you OK?'

'Yeah, but I'm just thinking that we didn't find anything useful that might help Eddie.'

Jed nodded, his mood becoming more sombre. 'Yeah, and I was so sure. Well, it's back to the drawing board then.'

'Yep. I suppose it is.' It seemed that the truth remained tantalisingly beyond their reach, despite their best efforts.

Chapter 21

Jed was feeling irritated and fractious. He has been so sure that they would find something in the shipping container, but in the end, there was nothing of any importance. He had dropped Imogen off and been unable to sleep with the information that swirled fruitlessly round his brain. He could draw no useful conclusions from any of the information they had gleaned. Geraldine and Eddie were seemingly having an affair, but apart from making them susceptible to blackmail, it didn't help him identify who the blackmailer was.

The next day he was riding out for Lydia Fox before riding at Wetherby. As he drove to Lydia's place, he slowed down past Hugh Mitchell's yard. He was as sure as he could be that Hugh wouldn't have seen them last night, he was far too drunk for that, so he took the opportunity to call in to meet Hugh properly. Perhaps, Hugh could shed some light on what had happened to Gary McKay, his missing stable jockey?

Anton looked up and frowned as Jed walked into the yard.

'Hi. I didn't get to meet Mr Mitchell last time and as I'm going to be riding for him, I thought I'd better introduce myself. I don't like riding for people I don't know.'

Anton looked perplexed and was about to speak when a large middle-aged man appeared from one of the stables. Jed recognised him from last night, the paunch, unruly brown and grey hair looked marginally neater than it did last night, but it was unmistakeably the same man.

'Hi. I'm Jed Cavendish. I'm taking some of your rides and have done some schooling for you. So, I thought I'd pop in as I was passing. I don't think you were here when I rode last time.'

Hugh took Jed's outstretched hand. 'Oh, right, Jed. Delighted to meet you.' The tone was cultured and suggested generations of privilege, certainly Eton or Harrow. Jed should know because he was from the same set, but the alcohol fumes coming off him were still strong, even at this time of the morning. Jed noticed that Hugh had the beginnings of a cauliflower nose and his eyes were bloodshot. His hand trembled a little as Jed shook it. He looked like a posh wino, with his shabby appearance.

'Come into the house for a coffee whilst we have a chat.'

The farmhouse kitchen was untidy with a stack of dirty pots overflowing in the sink, pizza boxes and takeaway cartons littered the table and a stack of wine bottles lined up by the bin. Cote de Nuit, he presumed.

'Sorry about the mess.' Hugh flicked on the kettle and washed up two mugs. 'Truth is since the missus left, it's all been getting a bit on top of me. Even my usual jockey, Gary, left me high and dry. No idea what happened to him. Even rang the police about him, got concerned ...'

Jed sipped his drink. 'Yes, I heard he'd upped and left. Any idea what happened to him?' He wondered if Gary's disappearance coincided with Hugh's wife leaving and wondered if Hugh had thought that too? Had they disappeared together? Probably, the two incidents were unrelated, he decided. He couldn't see Gary as a lothario, somehow.

Hugh shrugged. 'No. The police chaps weren't much help either. People go missing all the time apparently and if they're not vulnerable then they don't do anything at all.' He gave Jed a challenging look. 'I suppose you're going to bail out too, when you have some success, just like every other bugger…'

Jed took a gulp of coffee and stood up. He felt a flash of annoyance. He turned on he taps, squirted in some washing up liquid into the sink and began washing up.

'You don't have to do that…' spluttered Hugh, looking ashamed and rather embarrassed.

'No, too right I don't. I'll make a start and you can carry on.' He glared at Hugh. 'Look, one thing I do know is that self- pity and alcohol,' he pointed to the large stash of empty wine bottles, 'is a lethal cocktail that will not help anyone.'

Hugh glowered and began to splutter. 'Now, there's no call for that…I hardly know you and if you want those rides…'

'If **I** want to ride for you, I think you mean, then you'd better get your act together. I have seen lots of friends end up becoming alcoholics, so I know what I'm talking about.' He suddenly had a brainwave. 'Have you had any hallucinations or anything like that, because if you have then you need to seek help as soon as possible. It really is a slippery slope…'

Hugh coloured up. 'Well, now you mention it, two thieves appeared out of my storage container last night, but when I went back nothing had been stolen, so I'm beginning to think I imagined the whole thing.'

Jed nodded. He fished in his pocket for his phone and tapped a few keys. 'Hallucinations are really a sign that you're losing it. Right, here's the number for the local Alcoholics Anonymous, I think you should go as soon as possible.'

'Well, there's no need for that. It's just a bad patch, that's all… Besides, I am NOT an alcoholic.'

Jed continued to work through the pile of plates.

'And I'm no psychologist, but isn't that what they all say?' He pointed at the collection of about a dozen wine bottles, interspersed with the odd whiskey bottles. 'It's just a question of semantics. What is clear is that you have a problem with alcohol now and believe me that is no way to get your wife back.'

Hugh scowled and then looked hopeful.

'Do you think she will come back?' The hope in his eyes was pitiful.

Jed shrugged. 'I have no idea, but if you don't try and win her back then you'll never forgive yourself.' Just then he noticed a heap of invoices with a business card on top with the familiar black and yellow lorry logo. *LDF Horse Transport- for all your horses' needs.*

He pointed at the card remembering that he had seen it before.

'Do you use them? They seem to be making something of a name for themselves.'

Hugh shrugged. 'Yep. We often share with other trainers round here. Lydia, just up the road, Alistair Broadie, in the next village, quite a few of us use them. They are pretty good and efficient. Why?'

'No reason.' Jed had no idea if it was relevant or not, but he filed away the information somewhere in the recesses of his brain. He glanced at his watch.

'Now, that looks better, doesn't it? Don't forget what I said about the AA. Right, got to dash.'

He turned on his heel and walked away, leaving Hugh Mitchell open mouthed. It may have been professional suicide, but it felt good. It just sickened him to see such a great setup and talented horses being laid to waste, but more than that, it was the self-pity Hugh had displayed. He was so blinded by alcohol and his 'woe is me' attitude that he had no idea what Gary and the other gang members were up to and because of this, his friend, Eddie, lay in a coma. Hugh drank stupidly expensive wine to drown his sorrows when he had a good future ahead of him. Lydia would give her eye teeth for an opportunity like he had. Instead of making the most of it, he was allowing a man who spoke almost no English to run his yard. A sudden thought occurred to him. Was Anton involved? He decided that it was unlikely as his English was just too poor and that would be a huge handicap, unless he pretended not to speak English and it was all a ruse. Anton did have access to the horses and maybe he arranged the entries for the horses, given Hugh's problems? He wondered if he would hear from Hugh again and decided he didn't much care either way.

He arrived at Lydia's to find her nowhere to be seen. He wandered around and noticed that the whole place looked tidy, but even more run down and there were even less horses than on his previous visits. It was such a marked contrast from Hugh's place that he felt angry all over again. There was absolutely no one there, he noted, surprised as she seemed to have more staff when he last visited. Things must be a lot worse than he thought. He glanced at his watch, wondering how long he could wait. He was just stroking Just A Minute when Lydia appeared. She beamed as soon as she saw him.

'Oh hi. How are you? Hope you haven't been waiting long, I've just fixing my hurdles.' She held a hammer and a box of nails aloft.

'Oh, I could have helped you with that. Do you need anything else fixing?'

Lydia shook her head. 'No, it's fine. I just bashed in some nails, that's all. It wasn't hard.'

Jed grinned. 'I suppose so, but honestly if you need some muscle, I'll help.' He flexed his biceps like a weightlifter, which made Lydia smile. 'So, which horse do you want me to ride?'

'Since you're riding Just a Minute in a couple of weeks why don't you try him?'

After a few circuits of the gallops and several circuits jumping the hurdles, which Jed couldn't help but notice looked perfect, they were done. His mood lifted. Just a Minute was shaping up well and they discussed various races that Lydia was considering entering him in. Jed rode the chestnut back whilst Lydia walked on foot. Suddenly, her mobile phone trilled into action. Lydia frowned and hung back jabbering away in what sounded like French. Jed had wanted to talk to her about meeting Hugh Mitchell, but this distracted him.

'Hello. Oh, bonjour.' She looked a little uncomfortable. 'Je ne peux pas parler maintenant. Il est ici. Je t'appellerai plus tard. Ecoutez-moi, il est ici.' She stressed the last words and rang off.

'Hey, I'd no idea you could speak such good French. I'm impressed.'

Lydia flushed and shrugged. 'Well, it's just schoolgirl stuff. I have some friends coming over soon from Paris.'

Jed nodded taking this in.

'Well, you should help Anton some time.' Jed watched a variety of emotions flicker over her face. He hadn't asked for an explanation, but he didn't for one moment believe the one that Lydia had given him. He was sure that she had been talking to Anton. He was no linguist, but even he knew the words *il est ici*. He is here. They were talking about him. He wondered why Lydia had just lied to him? How well did she know Anton du Pre?

Jed checked on Eddie's condition, there was no change, texted Imogen and drove to Wetherby. He was riding a few horses, a couple for Kieron McLoughlin, one for Niall Curly and another for the permit holder Alastair Broadie in the fifth race. He followed Jake Horton into the weighing room and noticed that he took a last-minute call, and then scowled ominously. As usual the chatter in the weighing room kept him entertained. It was the other reason he loved racing, the first was the thrill of racing, the sheer adrenalin buzz of hurtling over fence after fence, the second was the camaraderie amongst the other men mad enough to love it too. All the chatter was about the fact that Felicity Hill was here at Wetherby. Whatever Jed thought about her interviewing skills and knowledge of horses, she certainly had generated a huge interest in racing and viewing figures as well as crowds at the races, were on the rise.

'You'd reckon lover boy might be a bit more bloody cheerful with his girlfriend being here,' commented Charlie Durrant, nodding at Jake Horton. 'He looks like he's got the weight of the world on his shoulders. Hey, what's up, Jake?'

Jake looked almost dazed. Jed noticed that his eyes were bloodshot, his face grey and his whole body literally sagged.

'P'raps he's had a row with Felicity,' suggested Tristan Davies. 'Poor bloke.'

Jed couldn't help but compare the man before them with the one a few days ago who had the whole weighing room agog with tales of the glittering parties he'd attended with Felicity. It did seem the most likely scenario, but there was something else in his whole demeanour. He looked almost as though he was afraid. Jed thought back to the party and tried to make sense of what he had seen there and Jake's presentation now. What the hell was going on?

Tristan shook his head. 'Well, he can't say we didn't warn him it was going to end in tears, poor guy.'

Thoughts about Jake's woes soon diminished as Jed rode. Kieron's two runners made a good show of things, one came in fourth and the other second. Kieron was delighted and clapped him on the back. His wife Geraldine was also at the races looking tense and unhappy. She glanced at Jed. He really wished he had the chance to talk to her on her own. He was sure that she must hold some useful information about what had happened to Eddie and who might be involved. She might not even know that it was significant, but he could really do with talking to her.

'You must come around to our place and do some schooling,' suggested Kieron.

Jed looked at Geraldine. She had dark shadows under her eyes, and her whole face was etched with tension. Poor woman, she must be going through hell.

'Great stuff. I'll give you a bell,' Jed replied, thinking it might be a good opportunity to talk to Geraldine.

Niall Curly's horse, Gazelle, sure as hell didn't jump like one, was Jed's first thought at he tried to correct the horse's stride coming up to the third hurdle. Gazelle pecked on landing and Jed had to cling on to avoid being unseated. Towards the end of the race he had managed to negotiate with the horse about its striding and they finished mid field. He explained to Niall that the horse needed a lot of schooling but had potential.

Jed didn't have high hopes of his ride in the last race, but he liked Alistair Broadie, the tall trainer he met in the parade ring, on sight. He had a calm, gentleness about him and radiated decency. It was still possible for small yard owners, usually monied farmers, to become permit holders, which meant that they could train horses for themselves and their family, so long as it wasn't on a commercial basis. Alastair explained that he farmed in Lincolnshire and had a few horses, one of which was Mother's Ruin. The bay was a handsome enough type, but he guessed that the horse would very likely be inexperienced. Besides, Jake Horton's mount Caboodle was the red-hot favourite. He watched as Jake spoke with the owners and the trainer. Jake still looked morose and depressed even when he was riding the likely winner. Some people didn't know when they were well off, he decided. Jake was staring into the crowd who had gathered round the parade ring. Jed followed his gaze and jolted with surprise at the person Jake's gaze was trained on. It was none other than the ex jockey, Darren Francis. He was a small, blond man who had been jailed for betting which was strictly prohibited for jockeys. There was also a cocaine habit that had fuelled the betting. Pity. He had thrown away a very promising career. Jed didn't realise that Darren and Jake knew each other. But it was the intensity of Darren's glare that drew Jed. Still, Darren was probably envious of Jake's burgeoning success, it probably made him reflect on his own foolishness, Jed decided.

Mother's Ruin had been surprisingly well schooled and as he got the measure of the horse, he was positioned midway down the field with another circuit to go. The horse jumped well and seemed full of running. Perhaps, he had done Alastair a disservice, he decided. He spotted Jake Horton's bright purple and black hooped cap in about fourth place and thought the race was likely to turn out true to form. A win might even cheer Jake up.

Jed wiped his mud-spattered goggles and decided to move into a gap on the inside rails as his mount showed no sign of tiring. Jed showed his horse the whip and they pinged over the third last edging up the field. Tristan Davies's horse had pecked badly and fell behind. The front runners were starting to fade, and he found to his surprise that he was in third position coming up last fence with Jake just ahead and Charlie Durrant's horse ahead of him, but tiring.

Jockeys had to take their chances where they found them, and Jed realised that he had a good opportunity for a place if he played his cards right. He pressed his legs against his mount's side and Mother's Ruin responded with a massive leap over the last. They landed just ahead of Charlie's horse with the purple hooped cap of Jake's just ahead of them. He could hear the roar of the crowd cheering him home as he used his heels, and body to push his horse faster. He gave the horse a couple of cracks with his whip and saw Horton's look of resignation as they pushed ahead. He expected Jake's horse to come back at him, but in a blur of speed, mud and sweat, they went on to win by two lengths.

Jed felt joy pulsate through him and he punched the air. As he slowed down, he saw the slight figure of Felicity Hill rushing towards him, closely followed by a camera man. She thrust a microphone on a stick into his face.

'Well done there Jed. What a brilliant ride and a surprise winner for...,' she glanced at her notes, 'trainer, Alastair Broadie. Talk us through the race, will you?'

Felicity was dressed in an eye-catching creation of a tweed mini skirt showing off taut thighs with a tight leather jacket unzipped to reveal her large, tanned cleavage. Even from a distance he was asphyxiated by waves of her cloying, heavy scent.

'Well, to be honest I didn't know what to expect, but Alastair has done a fantastic job with the horse and he jumped like a dream. In the final furlong I thought we were in for a place and I was expecting to come second, but in the end the horse jumped brilliantly over the last and won comfortably. He gave me a great ride.'

Felicity smirked. 'Yes. You seem to have made quite an impact in your first season as professional jockey. What are your plans for the future?'

'Oh, just to keep on going and ride as well as I can. I'm loving it so far.'

Felicity beamed. 'Thanks, Jed and well done once again.'

As the camera man disappeared, Felicity looked at him through his lashes and muttered. 'Perhaps, see you in the bar later?' before sashaying away on her high heels.

In the winner's enclosure, he was greeted by rapturous applause and a delighted Alastair.

'Bloody marvellous ride. You can have all my rides in the future. I can't bloody believe we beat the red-hot favourite. Amazing.'

Jed's mood plummeted as he processed what Alastair had just said. Jake had taken a call as he walked to the weighing room. Whatever the call was about, he had seemed instantly deflated then he had ridden the favourite and lost. He glanced at Jake who was speaking urgently to his trainer who was no doubt demanding an explanation for his second place. Outside the enclosure he noticed the pale face of Darren Francis giving Jake the thumbs up. So that explained why Jake hadn't pushed on and fought back. He remembered that fateful day at Uttoxeter when he intercepted Eddie's phone and didn't pass on the message *twelve in the sixth.* It was happening all over again. His win had been too easy and now he realised why. Jake hadn't tried because like Eddie he had been paid to lose. Jed took all the pats on the back and congratulations because it would have been churlish to do anything else, but inside he felt cheated and angry. Of course, he had taken Gary Mackay's place, so what had he expected? Now, more than ever, had to find out what was going on now because *he* had been affected. He had won the race under false pretences, now it was personal.

Chapter 22

Imogen typed in the data and glanced at her watch. She had been working solidly for three hours and it was now time for a break. She had a student coming in after lunch, so she decided to eat on the run and continue her research into Eddie's situation. Like Jed she felt frustrated at the lack of progress. Jed's hunch about the shipping container had led them down a blind alley and she felt that they were getting nowhere fast. Geraldine was definitely hiding something about her relationship with Eddie, but other than that there was no other information that helped them identify the blackmailer and person behind the betting scheme.   She also felt that Jed hadn't taken in her information regarding Marcus's knowledge of the scam that seriously. OK, he had nodded in the right places, but then brought the conversation back to safer ground, as though he was just humouring her. Yet, she knew her brother and something wasn't right. He had chosen to protect the person who harmed him, but she knew he was scared, and this was almost certainly to do with the betting scheme.

She went through the facts of the case. All the winners of the suspect races had been from Hugh Mitchell's yard. One of the things she didn't get was, if Eddie pulled the favourite, how the scammers could be sure that their horse would win? In hurdling, a horse could fall, hit a fence, be hindered, anything really. There had to be some relevance in the race distances as they were about two and a half to three miles, on the long side for this type of race. Even as a racing novice, she had realised this.

She googled 'betting frauds' and began scrolling through the results. She reasoned if she could find someone locally who was imprisoned for some sort of betting fraud, then maybe she could identify who was involved at the prison. Surely the authorities sent locals to local prisoners? They certainly had in Marcus's case, there were probably rules about that sort of thing, so that relatives could visit and help with the rehabilitation when they were released. She had told her students often enough that conducting internet searches was an art form, as it was surprising what came back when you slightly altered the wording of the search. She found lots of information about old frauds in Australia and the America which wasn't what she wanted. She typed Yorkshire betting scandals and came up with a whole load of other information, but none of it seemed relevant. There was a knock at the door, and she realised that she had wasted half an hour or so and found out precisely nothing. She opened the door and found Duncan Roberts, one of supervisees waiting.

Imogen supervised about twenty or so students who were completing degrees in Biochemistry. Usually the issues they were concerned about were to do with pastoral matters such as their accommodation, finances and emotional issues, but there were also queries about general academic matters. Some students barely attended any supervision sessions whereas others kept in regular contact. Duncan fell into the former category and she could not recall him from last year. He was a second year biochemistry student.

'So how have you settled in this year so far?'

'Great.' He shrugged. 'The first year was a haze of alcohol and partying, but this year I'm going to really get stuck in and make the most of the opportunities.'

Duncan went to explain that he had only just scraped through his first year but had been working in a kibbutz over the summer and had decided that he had squandered his time at university. Imogen made some notes and was impressed by the young man's attitude. His experiences had made him really grow up, it seemed, and he had developed a social conscience. He had decided to undertake some voluntary work which the university encouraged, in order to widen students' life experience.

'I do art with some prisoners. It's great and so rewarding. One old boy fancies himself as a bit of a tipster and gave me a cracking tip which came in at 20-1. I won a small fortune on Mother's Ruin at Wetherby.'

Imogen found herself unable to breathe. She tried to control her voice.

'Oh, which prison are you visiting?'

'Hull. My family live there, you see.'

Imogen felt the blood rushing to her ears.

'Well that's marvellous. What's the person's name, I mean, I'm just worried that he might be a risk or something…'

Duncan looked at her in surprise. 'Oh, it's Lennie something or other. And don't worry they are all low risk guys and there are prison officers around so it's all cool.'

Imogen moved the conversation on to avoid suspicion, but her heart was thumping in her chest. This was a real breakthrough. Lennie. Who would have thought that a student would hold the answer to the question she had been grappling with? Perhaps, if they could find out who Lennie was, it would unlock the whole mystery?

After she had her taekwondo lessons, where she and Andy sparred, and he came off worse as usual, she went home and switched on her computer. She began her internet search by using the words Lennie racing fraud. Her heart stilled as she read some of the articles and googled 'images'. A few grainy images appeared of a middle-aged man. He was smartly dressed and was smiling into the camera. She felt her skin prickle with anticipation.

Jed had never felt so compromised. His euphoria at winning his race was utterly decimated when he realised that it wasn't a genuine win. He was implicated, involved now and it made it really personal. He had to find out what on earth was going on. What had happened to Jake? If Eddie had been blackmailed to pull races, then it stood to reason that Jake had been too. It had to be something to do with the party he'd been to with Arabella and the two girls who Jake was supposedly signing autographs for. Felicity seemed to know the girls. Was she implicated? She had been involved with Eddie and now Jake. Both of them had come to grief through blackmail.

It was Imogen's turn to visit Eddie. She met Penny Morris who was just leaving. She had recognised her from the TV and of course, Jed had explained she had made up a rota for visitors in his mother's absence.

'Hello Imogen. I've been telling Eddie all about what's going on in the racing world in the hope that it might help him, but I'm off to the races now myself so I must dash. Give my love to Jed, won't you?'

She was wearing her tartan skirt and brogues and cut an energetic if old fashioned figure.

'Do you find it hard going back?'

Penny smiled enigmatically. 'Not at all. Besides I need to keep up to date with what that dreadful Felicity Hill is up to.'

Imogen took this in and wondered if she ought to confide in Penny about their concerns regarding Felicity, but she decided against it. Still, it wouldn't do any harm to do some fishing.

'What about Felicity Hill? '

'Well, she's up to something and she came from nowhere. I really wonder how on earth she got the job. There's something fishy going on, if you ask me.'

'Oh, in what way?'

Penny pulled a face and tapped the side of her nose. 'That's what I'm trying to find out, but something is very wrong about her, mark my words.'

As Penny walked away, Imogen made a mental note to tell Jed what Penny had said. It also occurred to her that Penny would look far better with a makeover. Her clothes aged her and made her look very dated. If she cut her hair and updated her image, then she would look so much better.

She had bought some Racing Posts and downloaded some Tammy Wynette music, which she knew Eddie loved. She set up the small speakers and dug out her phone.

'Hi there Eddie. How are you?' She sat near him and held his hand. 'I'll read you a couple of articles from The Racing Post and put on your favourite music in the background. Jed told me you're a Country and Western fan, especially Tammy Wynette, so here goes, hope you like it.'

She continued to read as the Golden Ring, DIVORCE, and Singing My Song played gently in the background. She read articles about trainers, best horses and breeders.

'We'll find out who did this to you, don't worry.'

Was it her imagination or was there some slight increase in pressure from Eddie's hand? She tried again.

'We know you were pulling horses Eddie, but we also think you were made to. We think you were being blackmailed because of your relationship with Geraldine.'

Again, she was sure there was a slight increase in the pressure from Eddie's hand. Imperceptible almost but there, she was sure of it. She went to tell the nurses and text Jed, her heart lifting.

Chapter 23

They met in a trendy bar in York city centre. The evening was cold and wet, but Imogen jogged over the cobbled streets, desperate to tell Jed more about Eddie and the progress he had made. She had already texted him and he had spoken to the hospital and to a very excited Bernadette.

Jed was already there when she arrived and had ordered her a white wine.

'So, how are you? It's great news about Eddie. It was a great idea playing his God-awful Country and Western music. He probably wanted to come out of his coma, so he could switch the terrible din off.' He grinned. 'At least he's on the mend at last, the hospital staff think it's a great sign, but want to do some more tests apparently. They want to move him to a specialist unit.' He took a sip of beer. 'And Bernadette is hot footing it over again now her daughter has given birth to a baby boy. They want to call him Jedidiah, Jed after me.'

'Wow. That's really good news. I didn't know your name was Jedidiah, wow! Anyway, I think it might be helpful to get Eddie some more favourite music and other sensory stuff too. You know sounds, smells, things to touch. What smells would a jockey be aware of at the races?'

'Well, that's easy. Horses, sweat, dung, damp grass, muscle rub from the weighing room anything like that. I'll take in my riding coat before it goes in the wash. Anyway, I finally managed to meet Hugh Mitchell.' He filled her in on his encounter with him.

'So, he's an alcoholic? He hardly sounds like a master criminal, does he?'

'No, that's just it. I doubt he could train ivy up a wall, let alone train any winners. No, I think he's being used by someone, he had a poor grip on his yard and could be easily manipulated.'

'So, who do you think is manipulating him? Anton?'

'I'm not sure. Could be, I suppose. Mitchell said that he and Lydia shared horse transport and I noticed he had an LDF transport invoice. 'Jed looked thoughtful.

Imogen braced herself. 'I have some news too. One of my students said he'd been volunteering in the prison and an old boy gave him a red, hot tip for a horse that won. The horse was racing at Wetherby apparently.'

Jed looked uncomfortable. 'Oh God. I was riding Mother's Ruin at Wetherby. He had long odds, but he romped home beating Jake Horton on the favourite. I was thrilled to win, but then when I thought I had been the lucky recipient of a race fix I was furious. It's personal now, so we have to find out what's going on. Jake took a call just before he went into the weighing room and was really moody afterwards. Then when I watched the replay, I think he let me win. Mother's Ruin was way out in the betting so it all fits. Plus, like Eddie, Jake has been seeing Felicity Hill.' He looked mournful. 'I mean, I should have expected it, riding for Mitchell.'

'God, that's awful Jed. I mean, great about the win, but sorry about the circumstances...' Imogen was about to ask him if he had heard of a Lennie in the context of racing fraud, but Jed seemed on edge and distracted.

'Have you been here before? Only there's some pretty strange types...'

They watched as a couple of very dapper men walked past them. They were exceedingly well dressed, with suits and waistcoats and spotted handkerchiefs in their top pockets. Even Imogen noticed their plucked eyebrows and one of them was wearing eyeliner, she was sure. They were almost foppish. However, Jed's attention was drawn to a couple of men in one corner of the bar.

'Hey, I think that's my favourite steward, Richard Kendrick over there chatting to another guy.' Imogen followed Jed's gaze and watched as the men whispered together conspiratorially.

'Who's the other chap?'

'A fellow steward, perhaps.' They looked on as the man grasped Kendrick's hand and gazed intently into his eyes. His eyes blazed with passion. It was such an intimate gesture that Jed double checked to see that it was Kendrick he was looking at, not someone else, a woman who was perhaps obscured from view. But there was no one else and finally Jed understood. He grabbed his coat and motioned for Imogen to follow him. Imogen drained her glass and accompanied him into the chilly night. They walked on over the cobbles towards the cathedral.

'Jed, what is it?'

'It's a gay bar.'

Imogen laughed at the outraged expression on Jed's face.

'And? Your steward is gay. What's the problem? It's really no big deal these days.' She was about to lecture him further on his small mindedness but took in the shock on his face.

Jed gave her a pitying look. 'Look, that's really not it. I left because I didn't want Kendrick to see us. You see, it is a big deal if he is married, that's why it's significant.'

Imogen kept up Jed's pace as he strode on.

'Oh, I see. He's married to a woman.' She could only imagine what she would make of her husband's clandestine meeting with another man in a gay bar.

Realisation dawned on Jed. 'It also makes Kendrick highly vulnerable to blackmail, wouldn't you say? Maybe that's how there weren't steward's inquiries into those races that Eddie pulled, because Kendrick explained the riding faults away as he was being blackmailed.'

'Would he be able to do that? Wouldn't he be challenged by the other stewards?'

Jed shook his head. 'Not from what I've seen of the man. He's a dominant type and as the stipendiary steward, the others would probably take their lead from him. He is the paid professional after all.'

'Right. So, who are the likely suspects?'

Jed whistled. 'The list just got longer and longer. Another thing. I now must add Lydia Fox to the list. She isn't what she seems, that is for sure. She told me that she competed under British Show Jumping Association rules, but when I googled her results, there was no trace of her.'

Imogen realised how hard it was for Jed to admit this, as he always seemed to have the utmost respect for Lydia.

'Supposing she was married and competed under her maiden name?'

'Maybe…' Jed seemed lost in thought for a minute.

'So, if we add Lydia to the list, who else do we need to consider?'

'Well, Lydia, Kendrick, Anton, maybe your prison chap. And somewhere Felicity Hill is involved. She was always flirting with Eddie

198

and now Jake. And of course, she was at the party when Jake disappeared with those two girls. I'm sure she has something on him.'

'Why not ask Jake Horton since he's the latest jockey to be implicated? It's worth a try, isn't it? Perhaps, it is something to do with the party.' Her brain ached from sifting through the facts and trying to make connections. It was exhausting. Then two seemingly unrelated pieces of information collided and suddenly made sense.

'Did you just say that Lydia and Mitchell shared horse transport?'

'Yes. Why?'

'Who trained the horse you won on, Mother's Ruin?'

'Alistair Broadie who lives in the next village to Lydia. Why?'

'And does Alistair Broadie sometimes use the same transport?'

Jed nodded. 'Yes. I'm sure Hugh Mitchell said he did. What is it?'

Imogen was beaming from ear to ear. 'I think we need to find out who the horse transporter is and investigate the lorries... It's the common link, don't you see?'

'Why?'

Jed listened as she outlined her theory, his eyes widening as realisation dawned.

'Genius. Mitchell told me it was LDF Equine Transport.' He pulled out his phone and googled them. 'They are based in York, look. It seems like they have a small fleet of lorries kept here.'

Imogen looked at the address. With Eddie improving and the case finally coming together, time was running out. She glanced at her watch.

'Well, we've no time to waste.'

Chapter 24

It was a dark, clear night as they made their way to an industrial area of York where LDF Equine Transporters kept their lorries. Imogen realised, too late, that her skirt and heels were not the best outfit for prowling about in the dead of night.

'I suppose you have your lockpicks and a torch?'

Jed grinned and pointed toward the glove box as they drew up at a compound on the outskirts of York. Imogen hugged her coat to her as once outside the cold bit into her skin. Jed pulled on his woollen hat and buttoned up his coat as he shone his torch around the compound. The lorries and office were protected by a high metal fence with a large gate and lock in situ. The sky was inky black and there was no sign of anyone. Jed shone the light around, as if searching for something.

'Good there's no alarm, but that lock looks pretty bulletproof.'

Imogen took the torch and shone it at the lock whilst Jed set to work with the lockpicks, going through the same routine of inserting one then exerting pressure then another, turning and twisting as he felt his way in. Imogen trained her eyes on the lock and tried to keep her arm steady though she was freezing, and her arm was in danger of going numb. Even to Imogen's eyes, the lock was large and therefore probably sophisticated. Damn. A car rounded the corner its lights illuminating them briefly, but it was just a driver turning around and the car soon disappeared. Imogen realised she had been holding her breath. Jed continued to twist and turn the picks, cursing as he did so until finally the lock sprang open. Jed laughed aloud, and they opened the gate, close it to and made their way into the compound. Imogen shook her hand to stop the numbness and followed him, her heart pounding.

Jed shone the torch around the space, illuminating two large lorries with the LDF Equine signs in the distinctive yellow and black livery and three much smaller lorries. Damn. Imogen realised it was highly unlikely that they would be able to get into the lorries without the keys. They would have to try and get into the office which might prove very tricky.

It seemed that Jed had other ideas as he started trying the doors on the smaller lorries and looking for windows that were left open for the horses. Having no joy, he turned his attention to the two larger lorries and gave her the thumbs up, as the grooms door had been left unlocked. In the distance, Imogen heard the hiss of brakes and a vehicle door bang shut somewhere as headlights blazed into the yard. She hid behind a lorry and peered round as a man got out of a van to open the gate to the compound. Damn. They had left the gate closed to, but a man was staring at it, clearly realising it was unlocked. She heard scraps of their conversation.

'Didn't you lock the damn thing properly?'

The response from someone within the cab was indistinct.

Thankfully they were not suspicious and having opened that gate, the lorry advanced into the yard. Two men alighted and began shining a torch around the compound. Imogen had scrabbled beneath one of the lorries and looked around for Jed. She could just make out his outline under the other. Her heart was pounding, and her throat ran dry as she lay as still as she could, the damp tarmac and the smell of winter mingled with diesel assailing her senses. The men swung their torches left and right in a systematic fashion. She heard the tread of footsteps and the beam of light swept over the lorry she was hiding under. She strained her ears to hear what was being said.

'Can't see 'owt, I reckon you forgot to lock the bloody gate. Dozy bugger. Best check the lorries inside too.'

The man's companion swore under his breath. 'No, I never left it. I'm sure I locked it.' He sounded younger and rather unconvincing. Imogen hoped fervently that he wouldn't be able to remember if he had locked it or not. She waited under the lorry, as the cold November damp seeped into her clothes, her legs stiff from being twisted into position. She heard the clump of feet above her as the older man searched the lorry. She let out a sigh of relief, as seemingly satisfied, he waited for his companion to search the other lorry.

'Can't find nuffink. Let's get outta here,' he eventually called.

Imogen laid stock still for an age whilst they climbed into a battered van. It was freezing, she had cramp in her leg, but her spirits lifted as they drove away. Then just as they passed the lorry Jed was hiding under, the vehicle came to an abrupt halt. The younger man swung open the van door, training a bright torch light under the lorry. Had they seen Jed? She crawled out to get a better view, all her senses on red alert. The man turned to his companion and muttered something indistinct. He went around the other side of the lorry and she realised that they were trying to trap Jed. She had no choice but to break cover. She crawled out from under the lorry and tiptoed as close as she could to the younger man. She tried to remember her taekwondo moves, as she crept stealthily towards her prey. It was time to put her training into action. She thought about the time when she was assaulted and how she had promised herself that neither she nor anyone she cared about would ever be in that situation again. She had to make her move. His torch light guided her to him. It was lucky that the other man was on the opposite side of the lorry. She knew she had only a split second to act. In an instant she had grabbed a large pebble and threw it with all her might, so that it fell ten feet or so in front of the cab. Then whilst the man's attention was directed towards this, she placed her foot between his legs, tripped him up and hurled him over her shoulder. She heard his bellow of surprise. There was sounds of a scuffle from the other side of the lorry. She ran around, eager to assist Jed, but saw that he had floored the other man. They both ran hell for leather to the gates and then down the narrow lane to where Jed had parked his Mercedes. She heard the men recovering and begin to give chase, but it was too late. Jed tore at the gears and drove as fast as he could to get out of there. Imogen gasped for breath as they drove through the moonlit lane, back onto the main road.

'Bloody hell, that was close,' she muttered. 'What a waste of time.' Now the adrenalin had begun to wear off, she felt rather flat and tired. Why on earth did they think that they could crack a complex criminal case, where the stakes were becoming ridiculously high. They'd had a very near miss, Eddie was in a coma and even her own brother had been badly beaten up because of it. Perhaps, they should just leave it to the professionals.

Jed sighed. She could hear the smile in his voice, that gave way to laughter. It was a while before he finally spoke.

'Bloody hell, Imogen. Remind me never to fall out with you. That was amazing! All that taekwondo training paid off then. Very impressive, indeed!'

In truth Imogen didn't think she had done anything amazing at all. It was just a routine move, but it had helped them escape.

'I suppose so, but it was all for nothing. We didn't find anything.'

There was a long pause.

'You speak for yourself.' Jed turned on his interior light and pulled out a length of transparent plastic pipe, a large bag of white powder and what looked like a narrow torch. Imogen stared at the haul, wondering what it was.

Jed laughed. 'Look. It's all the equipment you need for milkshaking.'

He ripped open the bag and plunged his finger in white powder before tasting it.

'It's definitely bicarbonate of soda.'

Imogen grinned at him. 'Wow.' She picked up the torch and fiddled with the switch as the brightest of lights lit up the night sky. The beam was fierce and blinding.

'Bloody hell. Turn that thing off.'

Imogen did so alarmed. 'What the hell is it?'

'A laser pen.' Jed was silent for a minute. Suddenly several pieces of obscure information swirled round his head before slowly settling. Everything started to made sense. What did the guy from the gym say about exceptionally bright lights being visible on the road just before Eddie's accident? That was how they did it!

'God, that's it. That's how they got Eddie to crash.'

For a moment they stared at their finds. Jed was the first to speak.

'Well, at least we now know how *they* did it.'

'But we still don't know who *they* are for definite and now they know we're onto them. Did you recognise either of them?'

'No. I should think they are quite low down the pecking order. At least it was dark, so they are unlikely to recognise us, so that will buy us some time.' He didn't believe it and neither did Imogen.

They both sat in silence as they contemplated how long they had before all hell broke loose.

Chapter 25

Jed met Geraldine in a quiet coffee house in York. Even though it was a cold winter's day she arrived wearing a large hat and sunglasses. Clearly, she was worried about being seen with him. She removed her sunglasses as she sipped her latte and it was evident that she was clearly feeling the strain from the dark shadows under her eyes.

'So, you've heard that Eddie is making progress? There's some slight responses which is really good.'

Geraldine immediately brightened. 'Yes. I met your friend at the hospital, and she seemed to imply that Eddie was pulling horses which is absolute rubbish.'

Jed had expected this and went on to tell her about the phone call he'd intercepted and how following this he had forgotten to pass the message on and how Eddie had won on number twelve and then met with an accident. Geraldine's eyes widened as Jed described the photo of the two of them that they had found amongst Eddie's things.

'I suspect that Eddie was being blackmailed because of his relationship with you.' The blood drained from Geraldine's face and she muttered and made to get up and leave. Jed grabbed her hand.

'But the thing is Geraldine, Eddie might be in even greater danger when he comes round and can reveal what happened to the police, it's still an open case to them, don't forget, so anything you can tell us just might help him...'

Geraldine sat down again and sighed as though she had the weight of the world on her shoulders.

'OK, OK you're right. We are in love and now it's all been ruined...' The tears began to fall. 'Kieran would ruin him, he'd never work in racing again if he found out about us. Kieran would make sure I never got custody of the children. But I swear I don't know anything about Eddie being blackmailed to stop horses or any of that...'

Jed was about to say that from his knowledge it was usually the women that got custody of the children, so he wasn't sure that that was the case and the perhaps was something he didn't know about.

'So, did Eddie ever say anything about money?'

Geraldine swallowed hard. 'He said he was coming into some money and we were going to run away to France, to Chantilly to start a stud farm or something.' Her face fell. 'Oh God, that's isn't it. He was taking bribes, that's where the money was coming from. He said he was expecting a windfall.'

Jed felt for her hand. 'I'm afraid that's what I believe. Now can you tell me who he mixed with, where he went, who could have found out about you two?'

It seemed that once the floodgates had opened, Geraldine could not stop talking. Two more coffees and a slice of cake later, he had no more idea who 'they' were. They still had a bewildering list of suspects. He left a distraught Geraldine, promising to do all he could to bring the blackmailers to justice.

Jed ran into Jake at Market Rasen after a rainy meeting when Jed managed a fourth on a horse from Kieran McLoughlin's yard, another ran down the field and he fell in the sixth. He spotted Jake Horton who had been rather morose and quiet in the changing room, heading to the bar, so he followed him.

'Now then mate, good afternoon?' Jake was slumped in a corner with at least three double whiskies and ginger ale chasers lined up his expression already glazed.

'Crap day, crap life, crap everything. I mean why do we do it, risk our lives for nothing, I dunno, it's shit…'

Jed ordered a diet coke and pulled up a chair. He was amazed at how quickly Jake had become bleary eyed and self pitying.

'How's the love life?'

Jake glared at him. 'What do you mean, what have you heard? Me and Felicity are cool…'

Jed nodded. 'Great. You seemed to be getting on at the party last week…'

Realisation dawned, and Jake suddenly grasped Jed's arm. 'That's right, you were there with that posh bit of stuff, weren't you? Hey, did you notice those two young girls, only I can't recall seeing them after I saw you, only…'

'What?' Jed sensed there was a story here. 'Do you want a lift home,' he glanced at the row of empty glasses. 'Only you shouldn't be driving after that lot.'

Jake nodded, downed the last of his scotch and staggered to his feet. They made their way to the car park with Jed having to guide Jake at one point. He had reached the stage of drunkenness where he was talking excitedly, all rubbish about how he and Felicity were going away together and how great their life was. It was all tinged with despondency.

As the drove, despair seemed to set in and as they negotiated the narrow Yorkshire lanes in the dark, Jed found that Jake had become quiet. To his consternation, he saw that he was crying, great wracking sobs broke out of him. His words tumbled out in a torrent.

'It's alright for you, Jed, born with a silver spoon in your bloody mouth, you can have your pick of the girls, but Felicity is all I want, and she'll dump me if she finds out. It was those bloody girls we met at the party. There's only some pics of me and them and now I'm being blackmailed, Jed. You gotta help me, mate. The thing is I can't remember any of it. A bloody threesome, every red blooded man's dream, the night of my life, I can't remember a damned thing! I think they must have slipped me something. Maybe some drug. But it must have happened, copies of the photos turned up in the post!'

'Who, Jake? Who is blackmailing you?'

Jake looked at him with deep despair. 'That's just it. I dunno. They just ring with instructions to stop a horse, on the phone. I've no idea who *they* are…You've gotta help me Jed. I can't remember doing anything with those two birds and what's worse is they might be underage. I'm bloody finished, that's what, mate. I might be prosecuted, lose my job, Felicity…'

Jed had seen the girls and heard them talking about the easiest money they had ever earned, presumably Jake had been drugged and the girls had stripped off to look like they were in bed with him, the perpetrators took photos and that was that. They were then free to blackmail Jake to do their bidding. Jake had probably been completely out of it, but with a clever photographer and two other willing participants, it could look exactly what they wanted it to look like.

'I did see those girls. They said they were getting a lift back home with someone called Daz. I saw him drive them. Does it ring any bells?'

'Daz?' Jake scratched his head. 'Nah, unless you mean Darren Francis. He was there, least I think he was…'

Jed did remember him. Darren Francis, how the hell was he involved? Information was swirling round his mind.

Jake continued to howl. Jed patted his arm absently.

'Listen to me Jake. I think you were set up and I think I can prove it. But you've got to tell me everything…'

Jake's eyes widened. He hiccupped loudly. 'Really? OK…'

Following Jake's revelation, Jed called Imogen and they decided to find out more about the girls. Jed had been hell bent on going alone, but Imogen persuaded him that she would accompany him as she didn't want him to get into any bother. As they approached the house that Jed had seen the girls being dropped off at, something occurred to Imogen.

'So, what are we going to do when we get there? What's the plan because we can't just rock up and knock on the door and break it to the girls' parents that they've been involved in some sort of orgy, can we?'

Jed frowned. 'No, of course not. Perhaps we can just find out a bit more about them. One was called Chan, maybe short for Chantelle or something.'

'OK.' Imogen still wasn't sure what they were going to do. In the end, they decided upon a plan. Imogen would walk up to the door carrying a plastic collection bag that Jake had found as he scrabbled around in the back of his car.

'Just say you're collecting for 'Save The Children'', he suggested, pointing to the writing on the bag.

Imogen walked up the path towards the large detached house with a sense of foreboding. Strange that the girls lived somewhere really nice. What on earth would their parents think about the girls' behaviour, she dreaded to think.

She knocked on the door worrying about what to say, when she was thrown by the door being opened by a pimply youth wearing a baseball cap.

'Yeah?'

'Oh, hello. I am collecting for charity. Can I leave you this bag for you to leave your unwanted items in?'

The youth scowled and shouted. An older woman came to the door.

'Can I help you?'

There were a few shouts and squeals in the background. Imogen must have looked alarmed at the noise.

'It's just the kids…', the woman explained.

'Oh right. I was just leaving you a charity bag if that's OK. It's for 'Save The Children.''

There was more shouting and screaming. Two girls, chewing gum and laughing uproariously, burst out of the door. Imogen stepped back to allow them to pass.

The woman tutted. 'Hey, where are you two off to?'

One of them gave her a challenging look. 'Just out. We'll be back before curfew, don't worry.'

The woman shook her head as the girls left. She took the bag Imogen proffered.

'Save The Children, hey? Very fitting since we're a Children's Home.'

'Oh. How many children live here?' Imogen asked.

The woman looked at her and smiled 'Oh, about six of the little darlings, at the moment. It feels like twice that number though.'

Imogen nodded and said her goodbyes.

So that was it. She pieced the information together. Everything suddenly fell into place. What better place to pick up some vulnerable young girls to manipulate than a children's home? It made her suddenly very angry.

Jed was silent and thoughtful on the drive back.

'What's up?'

'Those girls that just came out, I've seen them before…'

'At the party I presume?'

Jed shook his head. He had watched them sashaying along the street, full of bravado and knew he had seen them before.

'Are you going to tell me, or do I have to guess?'

Jed looked thoughtful. 'God, we really need to find out who is behind this whole thing.'

They discussed their ideas, but so far it was all speculation.

'Of course, there is always another way we could flush the perpetrators out once and for all…'

Imogen considered this as his words sunk in. What could he mean?

'Go on, I'm listening…'

Imogen listened and had to agree. It was a crazy plan, but it might just work.

Chapter 26

Jed picked Bernadette up from the train station and dropped her off at the hospital. She was in a buoyant mood, enthusing about the baby and Eddie's progress.

'And did I tell you she'd calling the baby Jed after you? You've been such a grand friend, so you have. That girlfriend of yours, she sounds amazing too. You don't want to be letting someone like her get away.' Bernadette nodded coyly. 'Is it serious between you?'

Jed laughed. 'No, look we're just friends, that's all. I like her, but she's an intellectual and probably wants to be involved with someone brainy too, not a jockey.'

Jed surprised himself by saying his thoughts out loud.

'Oh, opposites attract, in my opinion. Anyway, don't do yourself down, you're a fine young man, so y'are. Anyway, I'd like to meet Imogen, at least. I'd know then what was going on for sure…'

Jed felt rather uncomfortable about the way the conversation was heading and deliberately changed the subject. He had forgotten that Bernadette hadn't met Imogen.

'Look, Imogen was talking about familiar noises, music and smells helping people in comas. There's lots of research on this apparently. So, why don't you borrow my riding coat? It reeks of horses but that's the point apparently. Familiar sensory stimuli really help, you know, sounds, smells, touch and so on.'

Bernadette wrinkled up her nose. 'Well, if you say so, I'll whip it under his nose and see what happens. Then I'll pop it in the wash.' She pointed at her case. 'I've bought his whole CD collection, so we'll try that too and the village has recorded their voices for him. His old teacher, all his sisters and brothers have helped too, his cousins, even Father Quigley has recorded something for him. It's beautiful, poetic even.' She paused for breath. 'I rang the hospital and they'll move him in a couple of days when a bed comes up. He needs somewhere that can help him with the next phase of his recovery, so I won't be troubling you for long.'

'It's no bother at all, honestly.' Jed's brain was in overdrive. If Eddie was being moved within the next few days, they had to act soon.

Visiting came around quickly, Imogen decided, as she and her mother went through the same conversational dead ends with Marcus. His injuries were healed, and he looked reasonably well, if not more subdued than usual. He appeared slightly uneasy and cast anxious looks round at the other inmates and their visitors.

'So, only a month now. I bet you are counting down the days, aren't you dear?'

'Suppose,' said Marcus, a little sulkily. 'So, how's life at the University?' Imogen noticed the hopeful look in his eyes and instantly felt guilty. Damn, she had meant to look at the vacancy bulletin again for anything suitable for Marcus and she had forgotten.

'Everything is fine, and the work is really enjoyable. I haven't forgotten about the jobs. I have looked at the vacancy list and there's nothing so far, but I'm sure there will be soon.'

Marcus half smiled. 'OK. I will speak to my Probation Officer too. He's been to see me and there are some training opportunities, so that's good.' He brightened. 'I can't wait for a Big Mac when I get out and several pints to wash it down. Bliss.'

214

Mrs James chided Marcus for his love of fast food and filled him in on the local gossip.

Imogen glanced around and saw the solicitor type with his usual visitors, the two young men in baseball caps. They were sitting quite near to them as usual and one of the men stretched out his legs and leaned back towards their table. Again, she had the definite feeling that he was listening in. Both young lads were small and slight, one much more so than the other. The man who was sitting furthest away almost looked like a teenager with long slim limbs and small hands and feet. Perhaps, he was a grandson, she decided, but with his face shielded by the peak of his cap, it was hard to tell.

As planned, she cleared her throat and said rather loudly.

'Well, we have had a bit of good news. Do you remember that jockey I was talking about, Eddie O'Neill? He was in a coma but he's coming out of it. The police are keen to interview him regarding the accident because they still don't know what happened.'

The effect was instantaneous. Marcus paled and gulped whilst the young man visiting the solicitor guy remained stock still as though he was listening intently.

'Lovely,' continued her mother, clapping her hands together in glee. 'It just shows the wonders of modern medicine, doesn't it?

Marcus glanced around him, his eyes eventually resting on the solicitor chap, then he looked away.

Mrs James continued with her theme of medical breakthroughs by telling them about their next door neighbour who had had a heart bypass operation and was now running marathons.

'Marvellous, isn't it?' she continued.

Imogen's eye was drawn to the young man sitting furthest away as he fiddled with his cap, but not before she had seen him tucking in a long bit of hair. Very long. The hand that was frantically shoving the dark hair up into the cap was very slender with shaped nails. It was almost as if it was a girl. She steered the conversation back to safer ground, her mind in turmoil.

Chapter 27

Jed was riding at Wincanton. He was booked to ride three horses for Kieran McLoughlin and a couple for smaller trainers. He reflected on the fact that far from annoying Kieran after not pushing his horse, he had actually helped by demonstrating a sound understanding of horses and preserving his horse to live to fight another day. In the weighing room, the lads were upbeat except for Jake Horton who seemed rather quiet, probably wondering what would happen now he had told Jed about his worries. He tried to give him a reassuring look. Besides, if everything went to plan, he wouldn't have too long to wait before they could flush out the master criminal. All he had to do was tell them about Eddie.

'Great news anyway, lads. Eddie is getting better and better and will soon be able to speak to the police. I know they want to interview him because up until now they haven't had the opportunity.' There were cheers and whoops.

'Fantastic, mate. I'll look in on him next time I'm off. I've missed the story, the blarney and even the bloody awful music,' explained Tristan Davies.

'About bloody time,' said Charlie.

'Wonderful,' exclaimed another.

Even Jake nodded and looked pleased. 'Is he still in the same ward?'

'Yep, he certainly is.'

'Hey, how will you feel when Eddie comes back, and Kieran takes him on again,' asked Tommy Brandon, a young conditional jockey.

'I was only ever keeping his saddle warm, that was all. Besides, I do alright.' He knew that one by one they would all spread the news and eventually everyone would know that Eddie was recovering and well enough to speak to the police. Hopefully, the news would also reach the perpetrators too.

Kieron's horses both were placed, Niall Curley's horse came in fourth of a from a field of ten and his mount for Hugh Mitchell unseated him at the second to last. Since their meeting, Hugh was keen to tell Jed that he had gone to AA, was trying to get his life together and bizarrely thanked him for what he called, 'the no bullshit, straight talking approach.' Hugh looked better and was now more in evidence at race meetings. So as Jed made his way back to the weighing room, he decided that on balance he had managed to achieve his objectives all told. Back home he rang DI Roberts for a long chat. Now at least they had some physical evidence to give the police, which hopefully would enlist their help in catching the criminals.

The hospital room looked empty without Eddie in it. Although, he would not be able to make a statement to the police, as Jed had told everyone, he was making very good progress and had gone to a specialist unit for further assessment. Jed had persuaded the staff to leave behind his 'Get Well' cards and the rest of the equipment beeped quietly. He slipped between the covers, nodded to Imogen to dim the lights, and pulled the sheets up almost to his nose.

'Best of luck. I'll be outside with the others.' She gave him a shy little wave and he gave her the thumbs up. All they had to do now was wait.

218

Jed was glad that he had brought along his phone and discreetly plugged his earphones in and listened to some soothing classical music. He fidgeted this way and that, inhaling the faintly antiseptic smell of the hospital and heard various staff members as they went about their evening tasks. Jed rarely had the opportunity to lie still and reflect, but this forced him to think about Eddie, the original phone call that he had picked up ages ago, at least it seemed like a lifetime ago.

Twelve in the sixth

Had he been wrong to pick up the phone to save their ears from Eddie's awful musical tastes? Too late now. Could he be wrong about what it meant? Supposing he and Imogen had just got carried away with coincidences and had made connections where there weren't any? Yet, he knew in his heart that he was right. Not long to wait now. He wondered about the actions he should take, whether everyone would play their part, how the people would react when unveiled. He wondered about Imogen and the growing attraction between them and whether he would do anything about it. Whether Bernadette was right and had seen something in the way he talked about Imogen to draw the right conclusions, conclusions he hardly dare admit to himself. Then he heard his phone buzzing and slipped his hand into his pocket to turn it off. It was time and all his muscles and senses readied themselves, as he waited for the inevitable showdown.

He could feel his heart beating as the seconds and minutes ticked by. He mentally rehearsed his actions when *they* came and prayed that everyone would be in place and that nothing would go wrong. His ears strained as he heard the dull sound of footsteps approaching, getting closer and closer. How many of them were there? More than one he decided. He braced himself as he heard the soft click of the door being gently opened and felt a rush of air as it closed. They were inside. He had calculated how long he had to wait for them to approach and counted. It was a huge effort to keep the rhythm and not rush. Ten strides he had calculated. 1,2,3,4. His muscles ached from the effort of trying to keep still. He heard one of them breathing deeply, as they advanced closer and closer. 5,6,7,8. He willed himself to stay still. 9,10. With that he leapt deftly off the bed, whilst at the same time the doors were flung open as a switch was flicked on, flooding the room with blazing light and he heard the sound of thundering footsteps. Someone shouted commands, a deep authoritative voice followed by screams and scuffles. It was a while before his eyes adjusted to the light as he blinked, taking in the two burly police officers restraining two figures. Imogen appeared at his side, her face white as she grasped his arm.

'Thank God you're alright,' she murmured. He hugged her as they surveyed their captives.

They were both lying on their front, one swore profusely, the other struggled like a fish caught in a net. He instantly recognised the face of ex jockey Darren Francis, but it took him a while to recognise the other figure, her hair stuffed into a baseball cap, her usually composed, open face contorted with anger and spite. She was swearing in a most unladylike manner. She stared at him, bristling with dislike. Lydia Fox.

Chapter 28

The end of the season when the champion jockey, Charlie Durrant was crowned, coincided with Jed's birthday. Jed's season had gone from strength to strength and he had finished in the top thirty jockeys in terms of winners which was an amazing achievement in his first year as a professional. Even his parents had warmed to his choice of career and as a result, were hosting his birthday party at Cavendish House. It was the start of spring and Imogen had helped him deck out the east wing of Cavendish House with its large ballroom and high ceilings. Imogen had always known that Jed was posh but was astounded when she realised he was actually the son of a Lord. Still, she had relaxed when she had met Lord and Lady Cavendish who were very down to earth and of course she already knew Jed's sister, Milly. The party was attended by lots of jockeys, Jake Horton, Charlie Durrant, even Gary McKay who had been persuaded to come out of hiding from The Isle of Uist, together with Hugh Mitchell, Anton Du Pre and even Penny Morris. Of course, the guest of honour was Eddie O'Neill accompanied by Geraldine. Eddie was still in recovery and walked with a stick. However, he was doing really well. He had accepted that he wasn't likely to ride professionally again and there was the BHA inquiry still ongoing into race pulling. Still, Eddie was delighted just to be alive and Geraldine had now left Kieran who had been quite decent in the end, so life had its compensations. The racing world was still agog at the scandal that Jed and Imogen had uncovered.

Milly sipped champagne with Penny Morris and quizzed Imogen on the details of the case.

'I still don't really get it. How did you work out that Lydia Fox and Darren Francis were blackmailing jockeys to pull horses?'

Penny nodded. 'Yes, how did you know? I always thought it was Felicity Hill who was dodgy, but never Lydia. How did you know?'

'Well, it's a long story. Jed picked up Eddie's phone and heard the message *twelve in the sixth* and forgot to pass the message on, so Eddie won the race. Then Jed smelt a rat when Eddie was involved in the car accident. You see, Eddie won on number twelve, Happy Days in the sixth race and Jed wondered if the accident was his punishment for not complying with instructions. The police thought Eddie had simply taken too many diuretics and passed out...'

Jack piped up at this point. 'So, he asked you to look at Eddie's blood result, I suppose.'

'Correct. And Eddie wasn't in the least bit dehydrated at the time of the accident, so that set me thinking and Jed asked me to help him find out what was going on.'

Penny scowled. 'So, you knew all along that someone had tried to kill Eddie?'

Imogen nodded. 'Suspected, yes, but then again there's a massive difference in thinking something and proving it.'

'So, how did you prove it?' asked Milly.

'Well, that was altogether more complicated...' Jed appeared at Imogen's side. By now the group of noisy guests had quietened, all attention drawn to Jed and Imogen.

'How did you know that Lydia was involved along with her partner Darren and father,' asked Jake.

'Imogen used to go prison visiting and noticed two men visiting a man who we now know was Lennie Francis, Darren's father. Imogen noticed that they listened to her conversations and the person Imogen

222

visited, let slip that someone inside seemed to know an awful lot about betting. Of course, we now know that the visitors were Darren Francis and his girlfriend, Lydia Fox. You see, Lennie Francis was running his fraudulent activities via Darren and Lydia.' Jed looked apologetically at Eddie and Jake. 'Lydia set herself up as a trainer, Darren did work riding at various stables and they found out things about people, things that could be used to blackmail them. Then they blackmailed them to pull horses.'

Eddie shrugged, his arm round Geraldine. 'In my case it was my affair with Geraldine ...'

'And in mine they drugged me and tried to frame me for having relations with underage girls. But Jed and Imogen proved that it was all lies.'

Penny was nearly apoplectic with rage. 'God, how awful! But how did you know Lydia was involved?'

'Because I'd seen the girls they used to frame Jake at the party and we tracked them down to a local children's home. I recognised them, but it was a while before I remembered where I'd seen them. It was at Lydia's yard. I didn't recognise them at first at the party because they were caked in makeup. Lydia offered them riding lessons, took them under her wing and they trusted her, you see.'

Penny shook her head. 'Young, vulnerable girls, how utterly immoral!'

Milly was still looking confused. 'But even if they got a jockey to pull a race, how did they make sure their chosen horse, the one they backed, won? It's jump racing for God's sake and even I know horses can fall at any time.'

Jed smiled. 'Well, Imogen worked that out. The races that were pulled were all nearly three miles, on the long side for National Hunt races. Darren and Lydia set up a horse transport business. This was an off shoot of Lennie's crooked haulage business. Lydia targeted local trainers such as Hugh Mitchell whose yard was adjoining hers. Hugh was ill and had his eye off the ball and Lydia befriended his assistant trainer and suggested they use LDF Horse transport, planned which horses of Hugh's would be likely to win and used milkshaking.'

Milly shook her head. 'Milkshaking?'

Penny nodded. 'Oh, I see. Now I get it. I knew Darren had started a horse transport business and that's how they did it.'

Milly frowned. 'Did what? How can giving a horse milkshake make it win races?'

Penny smiled. 'Well. It's called milkshaking, but it means giving the horse a nasogastric dose of bicarbonate of soda to prevent the build-up of lactic acid, so over a longer distance it would delay the build-up of lactic acid and improve stamina, but not necessarily their speed.'

Milly was still looking confused.

'So, it wouldn't make the horse go any faster just delay fatigue, but the thing is it has to be given just before a race so on the way to the races is perfect,' explained Imogen.

Jed continued. 'And that explains why the calls to fix the races were pretty last minute. They had to be sure that they had managed to complete the milkshaking en route, you see.'

'And the trainers didn't know?' asked Penny.

Jed nodded looking at Hugh. 'Hugh was depressed at the time and was an easy target. Then they turned their attention to Alistair Broadie a local permit holder because he also needed a horse transporter. He didn't have sufficient staff to travel with horsebox and was told that LDF would take care of everything. They even blackmailed a steward and he let them know when the British Horseracing Authority were conducting drugs tests, as they only randomly test horses for milkshaking.'

Hugh looked embarrassed. 'I was a bloody fool, depressed and drinking too much at the time and had the stupidity to employ an assistant trainer who spoke French only, just because his father owned a vineyard. He gave me lots of excellent wine, you see. Lydia also speaks good French and manipulated Anton, my assistant.' He smiled at Jed. 'This young man gave me a good talking to and I haven't touched a drop of alcohol since and don't intend to.'

Penny patted his arm. 'Don't be too hard on yourself. We are all fallible, all human.'

Imogen looked from one to the other. It seemed like there might be a budding romance between Penny and Hugh.

Eddie approached them. 'I'd like to toast Jed because it's his birthday, but also Imogen for helping track down the culprits and making me a free man.' He looked quite emotional.

Everyone raised their glasses.

'And you should take the job as Kieron's stable jockey too. Promise me,' Eddie added.

Jed had been offered the post after a series of good rides but felt disloyal to Eddie so hadn't given Kieron his answer yet. He wasn't the only one with a new job.

Imogen smiled at Penny who had had a makeover and was sporting a blonde bob, wrap dress and kitten heels. 'I'm sure you'll do even better than before.' They were all delighted when she had been asked to take up her old post. Felicity had been moved on to a job selling jewellery on a shopping channel, a job that everyone felt she was much more suited to.

'Well, at least her orange colour will be more appreciated there,' joked Jed. Penny swatted his arm.

Penny beamed, pink with pleasure. Even Marcus had a new job as a box driver for Kieran McLoughlin. It was early days, but so far, he was doing fine. Jed's phone trilled into action and Imogen was close enough to him to hear the gushing tones of Arabella. Damn. She was no doubt trying to get her claws into him again. Jed had moved out into the corridor to take the call. Suddenly, Imogen felt desperately sad. Everyone was moving forward apart from her and after the drama of hunting criminals with Jed and watching Eddie recover, it was back to earth with a bump. She had no idea of the status of her relationship with Jed, he was a friend, he was infuriating but she also enjoyed his company, she had even got into racing and found herself following the racing results. If she was honest, her life was going to be very staid and even quite boring now, but she couldn't expect to see Jed regularly. After all, she had no reason to see him and that made her rather wistful. Besides, Arabella was bound to stake her claim on Jed, and that would be that. She expected she would arrive soon, Jed would distance himself and let Imogen down gently.

Jed came back and put his arm round her shoulders, almost as though he knew exactly what she was thinking.

'That was Arabella wishing me a happy birthday and telling me about her recent engagement.'

Imogen tried not to whoop in delight. 'Oh. Are you OK with that?'

Jed smiled. 'Of course. She already knew I had my eye on somebody else.' He raised his eyebrows meaningfully. 'So, we've solved a major crime together, put away several gang members, but we never did get around to going out on a proper date, did we? So, what do you think about us going out? We were so rudely interrupted last time ...' His eyes sparkled. 'What do you say?'

Imogen grinned back in as she felt her spirits rise instantly. She hesitated but only enough to worry him. With his good looks and exciting lifestyle, then things were never, ever going to be dull. She couldn't wait for the next chapter.

About Charlie De Luca

Charlie De Luca was brought up on a stud farm, where his father held a permit to train National Hunt horses, hence his lifelong passion for racing was borne. He reckons he visited most of the racecourses in England by the time he was ten. He has always loved horses but grew too tall to be a jockey. Charlie lives in rural Lincolnshire with his family and a variety of animals, including some ex-racehorses.

Charlie has written several racing thrillers which include: Rank Outsiders, The Gift Horse, Making Allowances and Hoodwinked.

You can connect with Charlie via twitter; @charliedeluca8 or visit his website.

Charlie is more than happy to connect with readers, so please feel free to contact him directly using the CONTACT button on the website.

www.charliedeluca.co.uk

If you enjoyed this book, then please leave a review. It only needs to be a line or two, but it makes such a difference to authors.

Praise for Charlie De Luca.

'He is fast becoming my favourite author.'

'Enjoyable books which are really well plotted and keep you guessing.'

'Satisfying reads, great plots.'

Printed in Great Britain
by Amazon